Caught Up in Leaves and Vines

Jake Graham

For anyone who has ever felt like they don't belong:
I hope you find your place in one of these stories

And for anyone who ever felt dismissed:
I hear you. You're not alone.

Contents

The Cave

The cold ocean breeze blew her hair into her face as she walked along the coastline, pulling her scarf tighter as the rain grew heavier. The shrill cries of birds in the distance startled her, and she clutched the torn envelope closer to her chest. The wind was becoming more violent, and the cave was still nowhere in sight. The wind swirled around her, the coldness melding with the dampness of her clothing, causing a feeling of numbness to take over. The birds stopped crying, the night fell silent, and awareness took over as she realised she was being watched. They warned her about this.

She caught sight of the cave in the distance and cautiously stumbled towards it, taking a deep breath as she entered the dark hole, holding her breath from the sour stench and stale air that emanated from within. As she slowly inched her way through the dark, she ran her hand along the cave's rough wall, trying to find her way while she waited for her eyes to adjust. The faint outline of a large wooden door caught her eye as she continued along the rocky floor, stopping before it and knocking loudly. Nothing. She waited a moment before knocking again. There were sounds of movement behind her, making it known that she was not alone. As she raised her hand to knock for the third time, the door opened with a sudden jolt. She took a small step back as the crooked man peered at her from behind the door, his scraggly purple hair falling over his face. Looking over her he saw the torn envelope and the bands tattooed on her wrist and stepped aside to allow her to come in making sure the door was bolted behind her. The sound of their footsteps echoed as they walked silently down the long muddy corridor. Doors on either side were all closed and bolted. Occasionally she would hear noises coming from the other side of them.

Screeching, rustling, scratching, scraping...

The lights were sombre and carefully placed so that the light would just reach the places it needed to and everywhere else was left barely visible. Soon enough they reached the end of the corridor where the final door stood on its own. It looked the same as the rest of the doors, but she could tell this one was different. This was the one.

She knocked lightly before turning the handle and taking three steps into the room. The walls were lined with bookcases, and the only furniture was a chair and desk towards the back in the centre of the room. This room was darker than the corridor with only two lanterns to light the entire area. She could just make out a dark-haired man who appeared to be around the same age as her father, perhaps a little older. He signalled for her to come closer and held out his hand as she walked towards him and handed over the envelope. Her eyes latched onto him intently, as he tore open the envelope and began reading the letter, hoping to see some sort of change in his expression, but there was none. He placed the letter upside down on the table as he stood up, and walked to the door, instructing her to follow.

She had delivered many letters before, but none of them had been anything like this. It was usually as simple as finding them, giving them the letter, and then leaving. But not this time.

He walked hurriedly through the corridors as she struggled to keep up, the crooked man trailing behind them. They soon came to another door. This one looked as though it hadn't been opened in quite a while. The dark-haired man opened the door and they all stepped into a small circular room, almost empty aside from the three hazmat suits hanging on the wall, and a lever in the centre of the room. He began putting on one of the suits and instructed her and the crooked man to do the same. She knew now that if things weren't serious before, they must be now. There had always been protocols and regulations for them to follow, but she had never encountered anything this urgent.

Once the suits were on, they stood by the lever, and the dark-haired man counted down.

Three...

Two...

One.

Reflections

He watched the children running around the park playing, laughing and screaming as he sat silently on a swing away from the rest.

It was the same every day.

All the children would go to the park with their parents and they would play and he would sit. It wasn't that he didn't try to play with them. He did. It was that they weren't *allowed* to play with him. Every time he even spoke to one of the children they would either walk away, or their parents would usher them to the other side of the playground.

It had been the same for as long as he could remember. He didn't know or understand why the other children couldn't go near him, but he wished he did.

One day a new girl arrived at the park. She had just moved here. She didn't know anyone. She didn't know who they were or what they were like. Upon her arrival, she ran straight into the middle of the park and spun around. She started off slow and soon turned faster and faster, moving like a hurricane ready to destroy everything in its path until suddenly she stopped.

She was facing him now.

He looked at her, curiosity painted in his eyes. She looked at him the same way. A moment or two passed before she made her way over and settled in the swing beside him.

They began to swing.

No words were spoken.

None were needed.

He didn't mind that she didn't speak to him, and he didn't want to speak first for fear of pushing her away. So, they swung. That was all they did.

The next few days were the same. The children would play, and they would swing.

After a week of the same silent routine, the girl finally spoke.

'Why are you alone?' Her voice was dry and croaky as if she hadn't spoken in a while, as if this moment was a rare exception.

He studied her, questioning her motives before responding. 'The other children don't like me.'

She stared at him for a moment before continuing to swing, silence descending once more.

He wondered why she was quiet; she wondered why he was alone. Neither felt the need to ask.

***

A few weeks passed, and nothing changed. The children still played, and they still swung. The parents of the other children gave them strange looks and warned their young ones to stay away. The children joked and laughed, but they still swung in silence.

Everything was fine.

Then one day, out of nowhere, a storm rolled in. The wind was fierce, and the rain fell like bullets. The children screamed and ran for cover. All the children except the little boy and the girl. They moved towards the tower and watched the rain fall as the other children and their families left the park.

It rained for hours and hours as they sat. After a while, she spoke once more. 'Do you know why they don't like you? Why they run and why they point and laugh?'

He thought for a moment before he spoke to make sure he knew what he was saying. 'I've tried to speak to them. It's not usually the children that leave; it's their parents who make them go away. My mum tells me to keep trying but it doesn't matter what I do. They just don't like me. I don't know why.'

She turned to face him, and he looked as though he might cry. A thought struck her as suddenly as the lightning slashing the sky. 'What's your name?'

'Nicholas,' he said quietly.

She was certain now. 'I'm Laura,' she mumbled, her voice as quiet as his. 'Come on. I have to show you something.'

She stood and offered him a hand before climbing down from the tower and heading down the spiral stairs that led beneath.

This was one of the places the children played, so he wasn't allowed here. He followed her past the naughts and crosses and the counting beads, past the sound pipes and under an archway to a room with a couple of benches and a fun mirror.

She stopped next to the mirror and gestured for him to stand in front of it. He walked cautiously forward, stopping half a meter before it. He looked at his reflection and saw something that was not himself. He moved his arm to see if it was truly his reflection and the arm in the mirror copied him. He took a step back and so did the person in the mirror. That had to be his reflection. Even a really good imitator wouldn't be able to copy him that well. But if this was his reflection . . . why was it a girl? He started to cry, and his reflection cried too.

The girl walked over to him and enveloped him in a hug as he cried.

'What's wrong with me?' he asked her between sobs. 'Why did you bring me here?'

She pulled back and looked him in the eyes. 'There is *nothing* wrong with you. I brought you here because I believe this is why the children run from you and their parents don't approve. You said your name is Nicholas, yes?'

He nodded.

'Nicholas, I know it's hard to understand right now, but they don't see you the same way you see yourself. They see you as a girl, Nicholas. I know you don't see that, and I understand it. They see me as a boy. My parents named me Tom and it didn't feel right to me.' She paused, making sure he was still listening. 'I got my friends to call me Laura and they didn't mind because I was still the same person. But my parents do. They think it's wrong and that's what happened with the children from the park. Their parents just don't understand.'

He looked at her. Finally, he understood. The children didn't hate him, they just didn't understand.

They stayed like that for the remainder of the afternoon until their parents came to collect them.

They didn't understand.

He didn't need them though.

He had Laura.

And he finally understood.

The First Zombie

Day 1

Someone on the other side calls out for chicken and I call back hastily as I pull the bag from the freezer and place four chicken burgers into the basket before setting it in the fryer to cook. I throw the bag back in the freezer and head down to check on the rest of the products.

Just as I'm walking towards the product racks, the current shift manager calls out from the front counter, asking me to go tidy the dining area and do cleanup.

Grabbing a spot-sweep, spray bottle and a cloth, I head out to the tables. I start at one side of the main area and work my way left to right, wiping down all of the empty tables, throwing away any scraps that people have abandoned, and sweeping up the crumbs and fallen lettuce. Then I head to the side dining area and do the same, followed by the outside tables. Finally, I check all the bins, only finding one in urgent need of being replaced. After putting away the trays, I return the spot-sweep, cloth and spray bottle, grab two rubbish bags from wash-up, and return to the overflowing bin. I switch the new bags out for the old ones, and the ready-to-explode bag of rubbish bumps around as I carry it out to the skip. After throwing the bag into the skip I head back to the kitchen, checking the time on the way. It's four-twenty and I'm set to finish at four-thirty. Once I've finished all of my set tasks, I clock off and head home for the day.

When I finally make it home, I notice a scrape on my leg. I have a shower and patch up the scrape before binge-watching Merlin until it's time for bed.

Day 2

Tuesday morning I wake up with a sore throat and a splitting headache. I manage to haul myself out of bed in the hope that my headache will dissipate, but after two hours of sitting on the couch trying to watch whatever rubbish is on TV, it has only gotten worse. Luckily I don't have work today, so I take a Panadol and crawl back into bed.

I wake up to an alarm going off around eleven-thirty, though this time my headache is much duller and I am able to scramble out of bed in peace. I head directly for the kitchen, grab myself a glass of juice and some snacks, and spend the rest of the day eating junk food and playing Call of Duty.

Day 3

Wednesday morning I have work again. I crawl out of bed and do my usual routine of having a shower, eating a slice of toast for breakfast, and sitting around on YouTube for the remaining thirty minutes before I have to leave. I still have a sore throat, but at least my headache has cleared up a bit.

I go to work and carry on with my duties. I put fried food and meat down as it runs out, and clean up whenever I can.

An hour into my shift, I notice my sore throat beginning to tickle.

Two hours in, it's turning into a cough, only growing more violent with time. My shift manager sends me home.

I feel too ill to stomach even the thought of food, so I go straight to bed. What point is there in being awake if everything you do is met with discomfort or worse?

Day 4

By the time Thursday rolls around my cough has worsened greatly, my headache has returned, and I can't manage to keep down anything I eat. I'm scheduled to work at ten, but with the state I'm in I'd only get sent home again and I don't want to risk infecting anyone else so I call in sick.

I spend the majority of the morning trying hard to hold myself back from throwing up, but, as one would expect, my attempts are futile.

When lunchtime comes around I'm still unable to consume anything, so I spend the remainder of the day in bed and, despite having done bugger all for the past twenty-four hours, I am beyond exhausted. I feel weak to a level I can't begin to explain, but despite my weariness, I still can't manage to sleep.

Day 5

When morning finally rolls around after a seemingly endless night, I can no longer ignore the feeling of hunger clawing at my insides, so I drag myself out of bed and decide to make some toast. It's a simple kind of food, but it's small, cheap, and takes little effort to both make and consume. As plain as it is, toast has always been a favourite of mine. But today, as I take a bite, it tastes as if I have just shoved a handful of ash into my mouth. I attempt to take another bite and am forced to spit it back out. I decide to try something else. Perhaps the sickness is making things taste different. I try a snack bar, some chips and a strawberry, but they all taste the same.

Later in the afternoon, I muster up the strength to go for a walk. I get dressed in a pair of shorts, an old AC/DC tank top and my worn-out black sneakers. Since I haven't been in the best condition lately I figure it's best to go for a short walk rather than a long one. As I begin to walk around my block, I notice something feels different about the world today. I'm unsure whether it's due to my reclusive behaviour in the last few days and the shock of seeing things as they are again, or if something has truly changed in my absence. The birds still sing, the dogs still bark, and the children are still playing in the park, but something feels different.

I continue walking anyway. I'm halfway around the block, there's no point in turning back now. As I walk, I take extra notice of everything, almost as if I'm making a mental map of the different people and their habits. I'm not sure why I'm doing this; perhaps I'm just overly curious about the world after being shut up in my flat for the best part of a week.

When I get to the last stretch of my walk, I see someone struggling to put up a new fence. I make my way over and ask if they need any help. We manage to get it all up with no serious damage done to us or the fence, only a few scratches on our hands from points and catches. By the time we finish, I am beginning to feel drained again, so I say my goodbyes and head home.

It's only once I have made it home and in the front door that I realise I have blood on my hands, and as I stumble to the bathroom to wash up, I notice something. It's a strange smell and I can't figure out exactly what it is or where it has come from. It's the kind of smell that makes you want to find whatever it is and savour it.

I give up trying to determine the source of the mysterious aroma and wash up. I decide it's a good idea to attempt to eat some toast once more, as I still haven't eaten, but despite how hungry I am everything still tastes awful.

Day 6, Part 1: 10:27am

Saturday morning I am woken up by a high-pitched scream and someone banging on my door. I groan and wait a moment to see if I can determine whether or not I have imagined the sounds, but when I hear the knocking a second time I decide I'd better get up and investigate. When I open the door I come face-to-face with a young girl with blood on her hands and knees, and tears streaming down her face.

'Hey there, what happened? Do you need some help?'

'I-I fell over. I was riding my scooter and I tripped,' she mumbles between sobs.

'Alright, did you want to come in for a minute so I can help you wash up before I give you some band-aids?' I offer. 'It's just that if you don't wash the grazes they can get infected.'

She nods and I lead her to the bathroom and pull out a stool and a face washer. I begin to run the water to soak the cloth. It has to be just the right temperature. The cold will sting and the heat will scald; it has to be perfectly warm. She sits patiently, only a few tears remain on her face as I begin to carefully wipe the dirt from the graze. As I'm cleaning out the last of the visible dirt I start to notice something. That smell, the same smell from yesterday, has returned.

I feel a sudden pang of hunger and my mouth begins to water. I don't know what the smell is or where it's coming from, but it's delicious. I try to concentrate on cleaning the young girl's graze but repeatedly find myself distracted by the alluring fragrance that is incessantly thickening in the air. I continue to mindlessly dab at the abrasion and set my mind to figuring out what the mysterious smell is.

Soon, I allow the cloth to slip from my fingers and fall into a crumpled heap on the floor as I come to a realisation; that the smell isn't wafting from anywhere. It never has been. It takes me a moment before I'm able to believe it, but it's the only thing that makes sense. The smell is coming from the blood.

I turn my head and look at the girl, only to be met with a look of confusion and fear. She can tell something has changed in me and I know it's wrong, but the control I had once felt has been taken over and all that's left in the space it had been is hunger; undying and everlasting. All sense of reasoning has been ripped out of my mind and all I can think about is making my way to the source of the aroma that is now flooding my senses, and devouring it. I feel my teeth biting into something firm, but tender, and become aware that I am now gnawing at the leg of the young girl, and though there is a muffled feeling that this is wrong, I can't stop. I feel her warm, sticky blood spilling out over her leg and onto the floor, creating a small puddle of thick red liquid. She struggles and cries out in pain before her body begins to slacken as I tear into her flesh.

There's a tapping sound coming from down the hall, followed by a loud bang and shouting. I leave the girl on the floor and head towards the sound of new life.

'This is the police, please walk out slowly with your hands up,' a voice calls out. 'I just want to talk.'

I shuffle towards the voices, still drunk from the taste of the young girl's blood.

'Sir, we received a call from a concerned neighbour who saw a young girl enter your home. A statement was made in which they claimed to have heard screams coming from inside the building. I am not here to cause trouble over what may have been a simple misunderstanding, I would only like to confirm the safety of the child in question.' The officer looks up as I turn into the front room leading to the door, and he hastily takes a step back before picking up his radio. 'This is Officer Brooks requesting backup. I repeat, Officer Brooks, requesting backup.'

I continue to drag myself across the room in his direction as the remnants of blood dribble slowly down my chin.

'Stop where you are,' the officer orders.

I'm only a few metres away from him now and his scent is starting to reach me. It's slightly different to the young girl's scent, but a delicacy all the same.

'Sir, you need to stop and tell me where the girl is.' His voice is shaking slightly now as he backs into the wall. 'Urgent assistance required. This is Officer Brooks calling for urgent assistance.'

Despite his recurring pleas, I do not stop. I continue to move closer and closer to him. I am only inches away from him now.

'You smell so good,' I try to say, but instead of words, all that comes out is a distorted groan.

'Whatever has happened, if there's something wrong we can get you help, but you need to step away and tell me where the girl is.'

My eyes meet his briefly and he gasps as though what he's seen has shocked him, but before he has time to react I throw myself into him and take a bite out of his neck. He, much like the girl, cries out in pain as he falls to the floor. I chew and gnaw at his flesh persistently, only to find myself being interrupted when a backup officer arrives.

It's funny, I think, how the police will respond so quickly to someone who no longer requires their assistance, but when people actually need their help they are nowhere to be found. I suppose this is one lesson they were going to have to learn at some point in their careers, among others, and this might just be the perfect way to teach them. Of course, I'm not doing this to teach anyone a lesson.

The backup officer barges through the door and I pounce on him before he has the chance to witness what remains of his partner. The girl has woken up from her death and is dragging herself towards me. I apologise for the noise with another grunt, and together we tear into our new feast.

Day 6, Part 2: 6:43pm

After finishing off the two policemen, the young girl and I trudge outside to reward ourselves with whatever, or whoever, we can find. So far I have tasted the flesh and blood of no less than seven people. The young girl has tasted five.

Somewhere along the way, we managed to pick up a truck driver, who now plods alongside us. He must have gotten caught up in the fight when I had been struck in the middle of the street by an aggravated pedestrian. She hadn't been the first to attack me. Others had tried, but we'd eaten them.

It's always me getting attacked. No one ever dares to attempt to harm the little girl. What kind of monster would want to hurt a sweet, innocent child?

We continue along, the young girl, the truck driver, and I, in search of fresh meat, stopping only to fight and snack on the occasional poorly-placed passerby.

Day 7: 3:13am

Most of them are sleeping now, but I can hear the ones that aren't. They are the lonely people who walk the streets in the silent hours of the morning, but not for much longer. Corpses remain sprawled on the streets to show where we have been. Those who have become aware of the new world that's coming have gone into hiding, and those who remain oblivious have chosen to continue with their lives as usual.

Others were not so lucky, they never got the chance to choose their fate.

I can no longer recall the number of lives I have assisted in taking. I have been in quite a few struggles, some resulting in death, while others have managed to walk away with no more than a scratch or bite. I've lost track of the young girl, but in her place, alongside the truck driver, are three new accomplices.

We find ourselves outside a brightly lit building occupied by three staff and a single customer. The place looks familiar, but I can't recall why. Whatever it is, we push our way through the door that has been left propped closed, and shuffle hungrily towards the nearest table, occupied by a man decked in a flannel shirt and torn jeans.

As he sits there alone, newspaper spread out on the table with a burger in one hand, I realise that everything we have worked for until this point in time was for nothing. I don't question whether or not he has somewhere to be. I don't wonder if he has children or a family to get home to. All that matters is the kill. The only important thing to me right now is how it will feel to tear apart his skin, taste his blood, and devour him.

Kill, kill, kill.

My first bite is taken from the side of the man's face and the rest of the group lunges at the man as he screams. I leave my companions to feast alone in hopes of finding a snack all for myself. As I begin to make my way towards the counter, one of the staff members emerges from the back room. They try to speak to me as I hobble towards them.

'Fred! Hey, are you alright? Man, you look like you've had a bit of trouble. Do you need me to call someone?'

They gasp with a combination of fear and surprise and I know they have discovered I'm not here alone. They turn and head back into the kitchen and pick something up.

'Stay back, man. Whatever's wrong with you, if I can help at all, tell me,' they plead.

I continue to move towards them with more haste than before. They call out to the other staff members who are hiding in the office. The closer I get to the person the more they cry and the more desperate their screaming becomes. I feel the knife they are holding plunge into my stomach, but where there should be pain, there is nothing. I lurch forward and bite them, but before I can dig in properly to my new supper, one of the other staff members emerges from the office holding what appears to be the broken handle of a mop or broom. She takes a swing, hitting me in the head and causing me to stagger slightly. Picking myself up, I continue to snap at her as she backs away. Fear is no longer a recognised emotion for me. I have already been stabbed and beaten, nothing can hurt me anymore, and nothing matters more than the sweet taste of fresh blood.

Kill, kill, kill.

A faint reflection of light meets my eyes as she swings the pole at me once more, this time knocking me to the ground. I take the opportunity to go for her legs and am met with a kick to the face that leaves me on the floor several metres away. This time, rather than moving away from me, she follows.

Before I can manage to stand again I am pinned down by the third staff member half-standing on me as the second raises the pole into the air, this time with one end directed at me rather than in a position to hit me side-on. I struggle, attempting to shake the person off me so I can stand in hopes of their insides meeting mine. The worker that had attacked me mumbles a final 'sorry', looking me in the eyes as she adjusts her grip on the pole before forcing it down again right towards . . .

Flicker

Knock, knock.

It was subtle, but it was a sound she couldn't ignore. Howling wind blew fiercely in the trees surrounding the isolated house. A light flickered in the next room. She walked cautiously to the door and opened it slowly.

The wind stopped. The light turned back on. The front step was empty.

She peered out into the darkness, searching for anyone who could have knocked on her door so late at night, but there was no sign of anyone. No trace that anyone had been there. Letting out the breath she'd been holding in, she stepped back inside and closed the door, making sure to do up the bolt this time.

When she was seated again, back at her desk, she kept thinking about the knocking she had heard.

It's impossible. No one could have been out there, especially not this late at night. I must have imagined it. That's it. I imagined it.

She started to write again, as she had been before the disturbance, and a feeling of unease slipped like fog in the back of her mind as she became enveloped in her work. Several minutes passed and the sounds from before seemed a mere dream. But even dreams come back sometimes, and this was no exception.

The light in the other room began to flicker again. She rose from her seat and headed towards it. They started to flicker faster and faster as she moved closer to the centre of the room, and when she reached it, as suddenly as it had begun, the light stopped flickering. She gazed up, curiously and cautiously, wondering what could have caused it to act in this way.

Why was it flickering? And why did it stop so –

Knock, knock.

She turned to face the door, wondering if she should open it again. After all, there was no one there last time, she'd imagined it. A chill made its way across the back of her neck and she felt something flick her hair. Startled by the feeling, she turned quickly to witness the culprit. No one was there. Everything was still.

Knock, knock.

The wind picked up again, faster and harder than before. Turning back to the door, she made her way towards it. Unbolting the lock, she prepared to face whatever stood on the other side. She opened the door, and again, there was nothing. Again, the trees were silenced.

The light turned off once more, diverting her attention. As she faced the still and darkened room beside her, she heard a new noise: the sound of footsteps running across the wooden floor in a room towards the back of the house. Twisting towards the sound, her breathing heavy, she felt uneasy once more. Air blew through the open door like a breath on the back of her neck, accompanied by an indistinct whisper. She turned sharply and slammed the door shut, doing up the bolt once more.

Please, she begged silently. Please let this be it.

Every light in the house turned off at once, she started to cry as she backed up against the door. A strong wind shook the house, causing it to shriek in response.

KNOCK, KNOCK.

Something pounded at the door now, constant and unrelenting. Lightning flashed and lit up the room, and she could see every cupboard door and every single window resting wide open. The pounding got louder.

There's nothing there. No one is there. Stop this. Stop knocking. STOP IT.

Silence. Everything stopped at once. The wind, the shrieking, the pounding. It was just her and the darkness.

And then it wasn't. Everything was illuminated as all of the lights filled the house with brightness. For a moment she felt calm, she felt reassured by the silence and the light.

Until then she felt it. A drip landed on her cheek. Then another. Following the source of the drip, she looked up at the ceiling above her and saw herself. Her face held a look of horror and fear, and blood dripped from several gashes that ran across her body.

A shadow shifted in the corner of her eye and she turned towards it. She never did get a proper look at what it was. All she saw was the dark outline of a figure, and the feeling of a sharp pain making its way across her chest and abdomen as everything faded into darkness.

Finally, the knocking has stopped.

A Body of Water, Organs of Fish

The day I had my appointment with Edwina Baker was one of the most important days of my life.

I was sent to her by my endocrinologist to assess whether or not I should be approved to begin my medical transition journey.

All I could think about on the way to the appointment and in the waiting room was everything I'd ever read or watched online about the different biases people have that can make or break your approval, and I knew that if I got denied approval it would be years before I was permitted to try again, if at all.

One of the things I had been most worried about was that she'd find out I was autistic because I'd read about a number of trans people being denied approval for HRT or surgery because they were autistic. Because of this, a lot of people withheld that information when going to these appointments. I was especially scared because I knew it was possible I wouldn't even have to mention it to her for her to know. A lot of people with experience in similar positions seemed to just *know* I was autistic. They almost always figured it out.

I had asked my friend, Rosalyn, to go with me to the appointment, as I did with most appointments. They were incredibly supportive and had been by my side every step of the way.

On the way there Rosalyn had asked what the psychologist's name was.

'Edwina,' I said. 'She must not be on holiday.'

Rosalyn frowned, not understanding the reference.

I chuckled. 'Chicken Run. It's how I remembered her name.'

'I don't get it,' they responded.

'There's a chicken called Edwina. She gets taken and one of the other chickens says "Is Edwina going on holiday?"'

'Oh, okay.'

***

Edwina invited us in and introduced herself.

We did the same.

She asked me a few basic questions, general getting-to-know-me sort of things, about my family and if they were supportive, and what I planned to do if I did go on T.

Then she asked me to explain situations where I had recognised that I didn't align with my assigned gender.

So I began.

When I was in first grade, I got in trouble with a teacher because of the way I sat because my legs were slightly parted and I didn't have them crossed.

"Girls don't sit like that," she shouted. "Fold your legs."

I looked right at her, spread them further apart, and continued to eat my lunch.

When I was in fifth grade, my father took me to the supermarket to buy groceries, and we bumped into an old friend of his. They started to chat, and mutual friends were mentioned.

"We should organise a camping trip soon," he suggested to my father. "One weekend, get out, go fishing, get a fire going."

"I wanna go camping!" I exclaimed, with an excited gasp.

My dad and his friend both chuckled.

"This one is more of a 'guys only' trip," my dad explained with amusement in his voice.

Something inside me dropped like a freefall, but I just frowned and kept my mouth shut. That moment stuck with me for years.

When I was in seventh grade, we had divided health classes.

Girls stayed in one room, boys were moved to another.

I was wearing a dress and the rules stated I was to stay put.

The teachers began to talk.

"This is a thing that happens to girls. This doesn't happen to boys, so they don't learn about this, they're learning about different things. This only happens to girls."

They were talking about periods, of course. But it only happened to girls, and the boys didn't need to know. I didn't need to know.

So I zoned out.

When I was in eighth grade, my haïr was long, down past my knees.

"Your hair is so long!" People would say.

"I know," I would respond. "I can put it in my pocket."

I wished I couldn't put it anywhere. I didn't want it long, but they wouldn't let me get it cut short. They wouldn't let me get it cut at all.

No matter how many times I cried.

No matter how much I said I hated it.

No matter how many times it found itself in a knotty, tangled, unmanageable mess.

No matter how many times I got locked in my room, not allowed to do anything else until my hair had been brushed and was entirely free of knots.

No matter how many hours it would take each time.

Because my grandmother loved it. She adored my hair, she wished it could be hers, and so she did the next closest thing and took detached ownership of my head, and my father would go along with it when she told me I should never *ever* get it cut.

When I was in ninth grade, I got my first period, and I completely freaked out.

I didn't understand what was happening. I didn't understand why it was happening. They said this only happened to the girls and I wasn't a girl so WHY was it happening to me?

I stood near the lockers, bawling, unsure what to do because my best friend wasn't there yet and I couldn't tell anyone else. I refused to talk to anyone else. One girl, someone I had been friends with, stood with me while I waited for my best friend to arrive. When she finally came I was crying so hard I could barely speak.

I had to tell her because someone needed to know. But I was an only child who lived with my dad, and this was happening when it shouldn't be. How could I explain that?

The two of them figured it out and I ended up having to speak to one of the teachers. She told me I had to tell my dad.

They didn't understand why I was so scared, or why I was so shocked to find out that not only would this last for days, but it would happen again many more times.

I never told my dad.

I got my friend to buy pads and we traded them at school.

My dad found out months later when I had an incident at school. Everyone else found out then too.

A few weeks later he decided I must need bras and told his mother to take me shopping.

I tried to tell them both I didn't need this.

They both insisted I did.

We went shopping. I was uncooperative the whole time. We bought two. I think I wore them for a week.

When I was in tenth grade, I was friends with a girl who'd been kept back in our grade.

She was older and more socially experienced than me, and I thought that meant she knew the right ways to act.

Sometimes she'd tell me I was doing something wrong.

"You have to wear a bra," she said. "We can tell you don't, and you just have to."

It was barely noticeable when I didn't, but she'd told me I *had* to, so she must have been right.

The following day I wore a bra to school, and while we were sitting in science class one of the popular girls walked up behind me, brushed her hand against my back, and pulled the strap so it flicked back, much like a rubber band.

I'd felt uncomfortable all day, and this was the final layer.

It was so obvious.

I looked ridiculous.

I never wore a bra again after that day.

When I was in eleventh grade, I discovered a band I'd never heard of in a poster magazine. I looked them up to see if I'd like them and found out the singer had recently come out as a transgender woman.

I'd never heard of anyone being transgender before, but somehow it made perfect sense.

I simply nodded to myself and moved on with my day, just as I would if I'd read what country they were from. It made sense to them, it made sense to me, that's all there is.

But I kept thinking about it.

I kept coming back to it.

"This is a thing," I thought. *"People can be trans."*

This thought echoed in my head for months, louder and louder, until it clicked.

I understand and relate to this because this is me. I'd always known I wasn't a girl, but until I read about this musician I'd simply thought I was wrong, that it was a mistake.

Knowing she existed, and others like her existed, made me realise that I wasn't wrong, I just had to fight a little harder to be seen for who I was. She helped me understand that was okay.

When I was in eleventh grade again, after I'd moved schools to finish year twelve elsewhere, I didn't know how to come out to my new class.

My entire grade had known at my old school because I'd changed my name on a social account and someone asked a question on an anonymous question site and I simply told them I was trans. My whole grade was accepting and supportive there, but I'd known them for years. I'd never met this new class, and I didn't know how they would react or respond. I also knew that being open about being trans in the wrong places could be risky.

So I waited.

I waited a couple of months until I was close to the class, when I knew everyone and was able to find out what they thought about LGBTQIA+ people, specifically trans people. They all seemed like they would be fine, so I told them.

My teacher refused to call me a different name because it was a boy's name. I told her that calling me my deadname was similar to if I started calling her Andrew.

She never questioned it again.

'Okay,' Edwina said softly before turning to Rosalyn. 'How long have you known Nick? What can you say about the way his gender affects his experiences?'

Rosalyn shifted in their seat and spoke confidently. 'Nick and I met at a walk for equality, actually, a bit over a year ago. He was the first openly trans person I'd met. He's always just been himself and doesn't really worry too much about what other people think. He seems to have a very specific way of understanding gender, and I don't know if that's because he's autistic, but I know that can also make things hard.'

'Autistic? Have you been diagnosed?' Edwina asked me.

'It's complicated. My grandmother was convinced I was autistic a few years ago when I was in year ten, I think, and she took me to see someone to try and find out. Her report was inconclusive, possibly because she specialised in working with children, and I was in my mid-teens at the time. Too young for adult testing, too old for kid testing. She said it was very likely I was autistic, but it could just be a combination of a few other things. But then I found the report she'd done, and in that, she wrote that I probably was. So I'm not entirely sure.'

She gave a slight nod. 'What can you tell me about your experiences with dysphoria?'

'I often have a lot of dysphoria about my chest, but I think other than that, it's mainly society's dysphoria against me.'

'What do you mean?'

'Well, for the most part, I don't care how I look. I know who I am. This is me, this is my identity, and I shouldn't have to conform to what other people expect me to look like. I accept that, and I accept myself. I can look at myself and not make judgements based on my appearance, but based on how I have identified myself. The people around me, on the other hand, don't see it the same way. They make assumptions based on how I dress, how I look, the way I speak and stand, and whatever else they can possibly think of.'

'Alright, and how do you think going on testosterone will help with this?'

'Going on T can help me appear more masc, by society's standards. Voice changes, facial and body shape, facial hair. I know that the effects vary for everyone, and not everything is the same, I know some things don't happen, or they take longer for some people. But going on T would help with those things.'

Edwina made a couple of notes. 'Do you struggle with your mental health much?'

'I... have anxiety,' I responded cautiously. Saying out loud that I have anxiety always gives me more anxiety.

'Do you ever think about hurting yourself?'

'Uh... well, yeah. Sometimes. I just... I guess.'

She nodded. 'Do you think going on testosterone would help with your anxiety?'

I paused to think for a moment, working out how best to respond. 'Yeah. I think so.'

'In what ways do you think it would help?'

'If I could appear in a way that aligned more with my gender, I wouldn't get misgendered as much. Getting misgendered is one of the biggest causes of my anxiety. I feel restricted in a lot of what I do and how I present myself for fear of being misgendered, and my anxiety gets significantly worse when someone does misgender me. Like if being trans is an aquatic ecosystem, and being misgendered is external factors causing damage to the environment.'

'An aquatic ecosystem? What do you mean? Could you explain that?'

Edwina looked at me intently, and I began to explain

'Well,' I sighed. 'The aquatic ecosystem analogy is one of the best ways I can think of to describe the trans experience, and how transphobic actions affect us. The trans experience, to me at least, feels most easily comparable to an aquatic ecosystem, something like a lake or river or pond.

'These environments work best because there are so many things, so many different pieces, parts, factors, and details that hold it all together. They all work with each other and rely on each other functioning in a certain way to survive. There's water, fish, plant life, bacteria, and so many other things all existing in this space, all playing a vital role in keeping it all alive and maintained. If anything happens to something in the environment, if any of these things are drastically affected or taken out of the equation entirely, it will affect the rest of that environment. Some of these things will affect their surroundings on a small level, some on a much greater level, but all parts do play an important role, and damage to any of them can range from having small, large, or even catastrophic consequences.

'I promise this is going somewhere. You're both giving me this look, and at this point, you probably have no clue what I'm talking about, but I swear this is relevant, just trust me.

'So the way that it works is that different acts of transphobia would affect different things, and how much things are affected would vary depending on the severity of the act. Smaller acts of transphobia, such as misgendering, could equate to dropping a piece of rubbish into the ecosystem, or a small amount of oil. As a standalone event, this isn't too bad. It's certainly not good, but it's not too serious. However, if it continues to happen, it builds up. Too much rubbish or oil in an aquatic ecosystem can pollute the water and make things sick.

'As I said, this represents small acts of transphobia, which are quite common. One alone might not do too much damage, it might do a couple of things, make a few things sick, but not sick enough to kill them or destroy them. Maybe they can recover from that, maybe they can't, we don't know. But if it continues, they keep going, there are more and more, they build up and it gets worse, they add to that and things will be less likely to recover, more likely to get sick from it, and if it builds up too much the results can get worse.

'Other things, harsher acts of transphobia, such as vulgar transphobia or threats, could wipe out, or at least make ill, an entire species that lives within the ecosystem. With that species ill or extinct within the ecosystem, other things that depend on its existence would be affected. Every single thing in that ecosystem is important, and the loss of any of them on a significant level would have serious ramifications.

'More extreme or severe acts of transphobia, such as violence, could wipe out something more crucial. Perhaps not a species, but maybe even something the entire ecosystem relies on to survive for nutrition. Some of those things may not be so bad, and not everything would be as greatly affected as others, but that nutrition may not return, and, given the opportunity, it could get worse. The species that rely on that nutrition could be wiped out as a result of that.

'Other things, perhaps, constant denial and rejection of a person's transness and identity could contribute to losing some of the water out of that ecosystem. The ecosystem may not be harmed by little bits disappearing, but if too much goes, other things within the ecosystem are sure to follow.

'In an ecosystem, everything in the space has a role, and everything affects something else. Repeated damage or loss to things within that environment will not only affect those things directly, but also other things around it, and something else will be affected by that in turn. It's a chain of impact. Some of these play greater roles and therefore will do greater damage, some will take more of a hit than others, but all in all, if it goes on being too much for too long, the ecosystem will not survive.'

We all sat in silence for a moment.

'That actually makes a lot of sense. I really like that,' Rosalyn said enthusiastically.

'Really? God, I was so worried it would sound like utter nonsense.'

'It did make sense,' Edwina added. 'We're about done here. I want you to know that I'm going to recommend you be approved to move ahead with going on testosterone.'

'Really?' I asked, my voice barely louder than a whisper. 'Oh my gosh, thank you so much.'

She smiled and nodded. 'Yes, I think this is a suitable option for you. I'm going to give my approval.'

My eyes and mouth widened. I don't know if I was in shock, exhausted, or simply unsure how to respond. I just listened as she explained what she needed to for the end of the session, and what she knew moving forward.

Rosalyn sensed I'd hit a wall and had become overwhelmed, so they took in the information and got me to engage when necessary for the remaining few minutes.

When everything had been said, we thanked her and headed out.

***

Once we were back outside, the fresh air hit me and I was flooded with a feeling of relief.

'Wow. We did it. Oh my god. I got approved, I'm gonna go on T. I finally did it!'

'You did! Yes! This is so exciting!'

'It is! Thank you so much for coming with me, I couldn't have done it without you. Your support really means a lot. I was really worried when you mentioned me being autistic because some people don't get approved based on that, but it was all fine!'

'Oh. I didn't know about that, I'm sorry,' they replied.

'No, don't be! It's all good. I got approved. Gosh, this is so... Ahh!'

Rosalyn laughed. 'Right! What next? Do you wanna maybe grab some food? Cake?'

'Yes.' I smiled. 'Cake sounds good.'

A Banquet for the Outcasts

December 22nd

'It just doesn't feel right, you know,' the boy with green hair mumbled, turning himself upside down in his spot on the couch. It was three days until Christmas, and they had decided to catch up one last time before the chaos. 'I can't believe they'd just leave you out of Christmas.'

'I know, Fern.'

'I mean, it's Christmas! It's the time for families to come together and share a meal and argue over who forgot the custard and why three different people all brought cream and share a laugh when your uncle goes to sit on the camping chair and falls right through the seat and maybe even exchange gifts to say "hey, I've been thinking about you" even though you probably only talk to half of them once or twice a year.'

'Yeah, it's pretty wild.'

Fern adjusted the monstera leaf stud in his left ear so it faced up again. 'They just left you out of it. You, who ten years ago were stated to be their entire reason for gathering in the first place.'

'Listen, Fern, I-'

'And now you're all grown up and they have new kids, but that doesn't mean they had any reason to just leave you out of it. Not Christmas. Never Christmas.'

'Fern. It's fine. We've been through this. It's not like they told me I couldn't come or neglected to invite me. If it's that important to them to have him there, that's fine.'

'But they know you can't be there if he is. If they know, it's an active decision to exclude you.'

Ash sighed and pulled himself out of the beanbag in the middle of the room. 'They know I've said I won't go if he's there, I get the feeling they think I'm bluffing like I'm just being fussy and looking to get my way, but they're expecting me to show up either way. I don't think they understand I'm not joking.'

'But they know how he treated you, everything he did, they can't just-'

'Yeah, but they did say they don't believe me. They think I'm lying. And regardless, they made it quite clear they didn't care what was happening when they left me there.' Ash headed over to the doorway and paused. 'And they don't know *everything*.'

He made his way to the kitchen to gather snacks for their movie night.

'Well, perhaps they'd alter their stance if they *did* know everything.'

'They won't, and I'm over it. If they gave a crap they would've listened any other time up to this point. If they're still not listening, I'm done trying to change that. I'm moving on,' Ash called back as he pulled a packet of chips from the cupboard. 'And I'm done talking about it.' He loaded his arms up with their favourite lollies (jellybeans), a packet of lamingtons (some form of cake was important, okay?), a juice box for Fern, a can of soft drink for himself, and, of course, the chips, and headed back to the lounge room where he proceeded to dump the pile directly onto the floor.

Ash stopped in front of the couch and folded his arms, staring down at Fern who remained upside down with a huge grin on his face. 'Scooch.'

Fern giggled. 'And if I-'

His sentence was cut short when Ash dove to begin poking his stomach. Fern screamed and folded his legs down in protection, and, in his haste, rolled off the couch, landing directly on the bag of chips and bursting them.

'Dammit, Fern. Good bloody job.'

***

Twenty minutes, a bowl of chips, and a freshly vacuumed floor later, the two boys were seated on the couch, scrolling through a small variety of streaming apps in hopes of finding the perfect movie to watch.

'So, Ash...'

'Yes, Fern?'

'What *are* you going to do for Christmas?'

'I'm not sure yet.'

'Is there anyone else you could spend it with? Or will you stay home? You're not going to spend Christmas alone, are you? You can't spend Christmas alone.'

'I don't know, Fern. I haven't really thought about it.'

'Okay.'

'I haven't exactly had time to think about it.'

'Okay.'

'It's just that you keep asking, and I only really found out yesterday.'

'Yeah.'

'Should we just watch Ghostbusters again?'

'As a counteroffer, might I suggest Gremlins? Similar vibes, perhaps less familiar and definitely not as funny, *but* it is the right time of year for it.'

'Ah.' Ash smiled warmly. ''Tis the season.'

***

Half an hour later, Fern grabbed the remote to pause the movie.

'So Ash, I was thinking.'

'Oh dear, is that what that noise was? No wonder he misses the rules and ends up with an outbreak of gremlins!'

'What if we hosted Christmas?'

'Fern, it's a little late. Everyone's already made their plans and-'

'Not for them. Screw them. We could host our own Christmas. For us, and others like us. The misplaced, the lost, the queer kids whose families don't accept them, and those who have been neglected and cast aside for the comfort of cranky old men who reek of beer and sweat. Like a last resort Christmas.'

'Oh my god, Fern.'

'I'm sorry.'

'No. No, you're right. That's a brilliant idea. Though I'm not sure I needed that particular image in my head.'

'Which one? Cranky old men, who reek of beer and sweat?'

'Exactly. And perhaps we could give it a more uplifting name. Last resort is a tad depressing.'

'Yes.' Fern bounced in his seat for a moment and resumed the movie.

***

They managed to make it through the rest of the movie without interruption. This was a record for Fern, who found it nearly impossible to sit still or remain focused on a single thing for long periods of time.

'So, what's the plan?' Fern called out as soon as the credits were over.

Ash was silent for a moment. 'Could we even pull this off? Do you think we could actually make it happen?'

'Well, it might be a bit hard to let people know it was happening, but yeah. Why wouldn't we? We've made it this far, I think we can handle planning a single day.'

'Right. I guess. It's just that... I don't know where we'd start. There'd be so much to figure out and plan and organise. People, in my house. Strangers in my house. Me, cooking. For other people.'

Fern made a loud popping noise with his mouth.

'Why'd you do that?'

'You were spiralling. It worked.' Fern smiled. 'Listen. Calm down. For now, we need to work out if it's lunch or dinner, if we know anyone specific to invite, and what kind of food we want. Extra details come after that.'

'Okay, well what if-'

'If we do dinner, I can help. I've got a family thing for lunch this year, so I can't come for lunch, but if we do dinner I can come and help out and I might be able to bring some leftovers.'

'Okay, that sounds great, we can do-'

'I'll *definitely* be able to bring leftovers. There's always enough to feed ten people for a week. Plus, that way I can bring some roast stuff because we might get someone who isn't a vegetarian and won't want to touch whatever you cook.' Fern was bouncing in his seat again. He had a tendency to get over-excited and carried away when he had ideas. He didn't wait for them to settle, he just blurted them out like a reflex.

'Okay, you can bring leftovers. I might just get rolls, salad, and desserts and we can have a cold dinner.'

'And things to go in them.'

'What?'

'You need things to go in the rolls too. And sauce. People like sauce.'

'Fern, I bought sauce months ago.'

A frown formed on Fern's forehead. Tried, at least. He was too soft for such harsh lines. 'You did?'

'Yep.' Ash chuckled. 'You were here for dinner and wanted sauce on your chips but I didn't have any. You looked so sad about having sauce-less chips, I added it to my next shopping list.'

'AW, YOU DID? THAT'S SO SWEET! THANK YOU, ASHY!'

'Calm down, Fern.'

'Ooh, maybe we should get some cheese, too.'

'Okay, Fern.'

They carried on like this for another hour, and between spurts of excessive enthusiasm and bouts of hopelessness, they'd finally met every decision they deemed important. They would do Christmas dinner at Ash's house, Fern would contribute leftovers from his family lunch (permission in advance wasn't necessary, there was always far too much at the end), Ash would provide fresh rolls from the bakery, salad (the fruit and vegetable kind *and* the wet kind, as Fern had emphasised repeatedly), fillings for the rolls (including, but not limited to, sauce and cheese), and desserts (mince pies, for those after a traditional Christmas sweet, and sponge roll for those who didn't have the taste for tradition. Not forgetting custard and cream, of course).

They'd both messaged a few people and drafted a post on social media.

COME ONE, COME ALL!

Ash and Fern are thrilled to invite you to

A Banquet for the Outcasts

When: Christmas evening (not to be confused with Christmas Eve)

Time: December 25th, after 5:30pm (welcome earlier)

Where: Ash's house (pm for address)

Why: Nobody should be abandoned, dismissed, or mistreated. Especially not on Christmas. We want people to feel safe and loved. If you can't be with your family, you can join ours as we make our own.

'Wouldn't "Time" and "When" come under the same thing?' Ash frowned. It looked far more natural on him.

'Yes and no.'

Ash stared at Fern, waiting for an explanation.

'Well, "When" is like "When is it?" and "Time" is "What time?".'

'But you've said "Christmas evening" and then said "December 25th, after 5:30pm" and those mean the same thing.'

'Eh... They do, but they don't.'

'I just think it might confuse people.'

'I just don't want people to be unsure because there's information missing.' Fern's face trembled as he started to panic. He was far too used to being misunderstood.

'I think they'd know either way. There wouldn't be information missing. It's the same thing, just said a different way,' Ash continued. 'But we don't have to change it. I like what you've done, it's a good post.'

Fern looked up at him with pleading eyes and a sad smile, and Ash ruffled his curly green hair.

'Okay, I'm posting it.'

'Don't forget to make it shareable.'

'I won't. And it's up.'

'Nice work. I'll just find it and...' Ash sighed. 'Fern.'

'Yessy?'

'It's set to "Friends only". Can you... just give me your phone.'

Fern pouted as he watched Ash.

'There. It's shareable. And I've shared it. And now... we wait, I guess.'

'I guess we do.'

December 25th (Christmas Day)

'What do you mean you're not coming?' Ash's dad hounded. 'It's Christmas.'

'I told you I wasn't coming. I can't. Not if he's there.'

'Don't be ridiculous. Why can't you come?'

'Is he going to be there?'

'Of course. Why wouldn't he be? He's family.'

'Then I won't be. It's that simple.'

'You're being ridiculous. It's Christmas. The kids want to see you. You don't have to talk to him.'

'As I've said several times, if he's there, I can't be.' Ash's voice was firm, refusing to be swayed. He wanted to see the kids too, they loved him and he wanted them to be happy, but he wasn't putting himself at risk when he knew they'd be fine without him. 'I've made other plans anyway.'

'What other plans?'

'I'm having dinner with some friends.' He could picture his father rolling his eyes. Christmas was about *family*.

They continued to argue for a few more minutes before the conversation wore down to an end. Knowing he was soon to be bombarded with texts from various relatives, he turned off his notifications. He didn't need that conversation, and he definitely wasn't prepared for more of the same. Not today. He was already feeling overwhelmed knowing he had to host Christmas dinner. He'd never hosted a proper dinner before, and Christmas was a big deal. Why did he think this was a good idea?

***

Ash spent the rest of the morning organising and setting up as much as he could; anything that wouldn't go dry or spoil in the heat. As nervous as he was, he was pretty excited too. He'd found a bag full of tinsel, a nice tablecloth, and a few cute ornaments in an op shop and decorated the house with them. It was fitting, he thought, to use the decorations others had cast aside. There was a pile of wrapped gifts left unlabelled, some things he'd picked up when he'd been out, so everyone would still be able to enjoy a present and not miss out on another experience. He'd picked up a few books, some jewellery, a craft kit, and the most beautiful blanket. The decorations and gifts had only cost him twenty dollars altogether, and it was such a simple way to bring a few people a little extra joy and maybe, just maybe, put a smile on their faces.

They'd had a few responses, and it looked like they would have about five people attending Christmas Dinner, but they'd made sure to account for a couple of extras in case they had any last-minute additions.

***

Fern's mum dropped him off around four o'clock. Ellie had jumped on board the moment she'd heard about their plan. She'd even picked up a few extra things for them to make sure they would have enough food. When Fern had gotten home a few days earlier and told her about it, she'd called Ash and said "People might be treating you like scraps, but that doesn't mean you need to be eating them. We'll come early and I'll roast some veggies for you before I leave". If it had been up to her, he would've been going to their lunch with her family.

They brought everything in from the car, putting away things they'd need later, and setting the rest up as needed. Ellie got to work in the kitchen, turning on the oven and preparing the carrots, pumpkin, and potatoes on trays. The two boys walked around the house, going from room to room to make sure everything was ready.

'Mum got you a gift, by the way,' Fern said while they walked around the yard.

'You mean the veggies? I know, she's cooking them now. It's very sweet of her. She really didn't have to do this for us.'

'No, not the veggies. She got you an actual gift.'

'Oh.'

'She really cares about you. You're like the kid she never had. We're basically brothers.'

'I didn't get her one.'

'What?'

'Your mum. I didn't get her a gift. I probably should have, right? I mean, yeah, I should have. Shit. I was so focused on fixing Christmas, why didn't I think...? Stupid.'

'No, Ash. Listen. First of all, you can't fix Christmas. It's not broken, just different. Second of all, my mum doesn't expect gifts from you. As I said, you're like the child she never had. And besides, she didn't go looking specifically for something to give you. She saw something and couldn't leave it because it reminded her so much of you. Don't feel bad, just accept it. Please.'

'Yeah, of course, I-'

Ash was cut off by the sound of a car pulling up out the front. He frowned, pulling his phone out to check the time. No one was due to arrive for another hour. They ran back inside as Ellie stepped into view, an apologetic look on her face, and headed back into the kitchen. Ash's grandmother stormed past and looked at him.

'Come on,' she snapped.

'What do you mean "come on"?'

'Christmas dinner at your dad's house. Are you ready?'

'I'm not going. I told them I wasn't going.'

'I know. He did tell me you'd said you weren't going, but I thought maybe you'd change your mind. It's Christmas and the kids would love to see you.'

'I know the kids want to see me. I'd like to see them too, but not if *he* is going to be there.'

'You don't have to talk to him just because he's there.'

'I can't be in the same place as him. If he's there, I'm not going.'

'Oh, what does it matter? Can't you just get over it? He's not a bad man, you know.'

Ash let out an exasperated laugh. 'He's not a good man. Good people don't treat people the way he treats people. And besides, we have other plans.'

'Oh, whatever,' she huffed, rolling her eyes. 'I just thought maybe you could put it aside for one day.'

They stared blankly at her, shocked at how persistent she was, and her inability to see the irony in the way she was trying to pressure Ash to let something go.

'Come on, if you get ready quickly we won't be late.'

'UGH!' Fern yelled. 'He's not going. He's said that. Repeatedly. To you, and to everyone else. He doesn't need to let it go or put it aside, *you* need to respect him and his feelings. If you don't feel like you can respect him, hold on to your words until you figure out how to.'

Everyone was silent for a moment. Ellie had heard her son scream and was watching the interaction. Fern stormed out to the backyard. Ash was still staring.

'You need to sort your friends out and figure out if they're really the right people to be around,' his grandmother spoke furiously. 'I have done nothing wrong, and I do not deserve to be spoken to like that. I didn't come here to be yelled at or insulted, I am just trying my best. She was completely out of line. I don't think she's having a good influence on you. You were less argumentative before you became friends with her.'

'*He* is my friend and everything he said makes exactly the right amount of sense. I told you I wasn't going, and you came in here, to my house, telling me to get over it, and started pressuring me and saying I should go anyway. You're trying to force me to go along just because *you* think I should. No. *You* were completely out of line. And on top of that, thinking it's okay to misgender someone, anyone, but especially my *friends*? No fucking way.'

'Oh, I slip up, I'm old.'

'No. There was no reason for that. You have only ever known him as he is, you have no excuses or reasons for misgendering him and doing so not only shows you don't respect him, it shows you don't respect me either.'

'Have I misgendered you today? No, I didn't think so. See, I'm trying.'

'No, but you misgendered my friend in anger, and if you misgender him, there's nothing to say you don't still misgender me.'

She rolled her eyes and shook her head slightly. 'I mostly say he now, and I call you Ash. You know it's hard for me when I knew you for eighteen years as she and Alice.'

'Get out.' Ellie stepped in. 'I think it's high time you leave. You will not come into another person's house and disrespect them as you have done today. Ash has made it very clear he's not going with you. Not only that, you were incredibly rude to my son. If it wasn't clear enough when you first arrived, it's certainly clear now that your presence here is not welcome today. I hope you and your family have a lovely evening, and while you're doing so, you can think about the absence of this beautiful boy, and why it is that you'd rather put yourselves first than do the bare minimum to care about someone who is family, someone you should be there for, and someone you claim to love. Merry Christmas. Get the hell out.'

Ash held back a smile as he watched the look on his grandmother's face shift. He could tell she was refraining from continuing the argument as she silently picked up her bag, headed back out to her car, and left. Turning to Ellie, tears in his eyes threatening to spill, he thanked her as she pulled him into a hug.

'Sometimes, as much as it might hurt... sometimes we have to know when to tell them to go,' she whispered as she rested her chin on his head. 'I am so sorry. I wish I'd spoken up sooner. You deserve so much better than the way they've treated you. You are a wonderful young man, and I am so incredibly proud of you. Promise me you'll never let them talk to you like that or bully you into the things they want?'

Ash sniffed as he pulled away and looked up at her. 'I promise.'

They found Fern in the backyard, playing with a bubble wand, and called him in. Their guests were expected to arrive soon, but Ellie wanted the three of them to sit down together for a few minutes first.

'I'm so proud of you both. For doing this, and for standing up for yourselves today. You're both exceptional young men, and I couldn't have asked for better sons.'

'Wait,' Ash said with a slight tremble in his voice. 'Sons? Plural?'

'Fern might be my son by blood, but you're my son too. In my heart, and every part of my being, you are my son too. Never doubt that.' She paused for a moment before picking up a bag she'd tucked under the bench in the kitchen when she arrived. 'Here. I know I didn't have to get you anything, and, before you worry, it wasn't any trouble. But I saw this, and it was so perfect that I just had to get it for you. If you don't like it, that's okay too.'

Ash took the bag and pulled out the gift inside, unwrapping it carefully. It was one of those t-shirts with a joke caption on the front, but this one read "For some people, the best thing they'll ever do in life is turn into ash".

Ash's face broke into a huge smile. 'I love it. So much. Thank you so much. Wow, I...' He stopped abruptly, picked up the shirt, and ran into the bedroom. A few seconds later he emerged with it on. 'It fits perfectly!'

'I'm glad you like it.' Ellie smiled.

Before Ash could say anything else, there was a knock on the door. They welcomed their first guest, Jess, a friend of Fern's cousin, who had recently moved to the area for work while looking for a fresh start after both her parents passed away. The boys gave her a quick tour of the house and they'd had just returned to the kitchen when they heard the sound of laughter travelling up the driveway.

Ash opened the door to let in Bethany, an old friend of his from school, and her partner Lucas, followed closely by Ainsley. They'd met Ainsley online in a local community group, and Bethany had offered to pick them up on the way. Bethany's family had stopped inviting her to family events because she pulled them up on their racist comments and queerphobia; two things her uncle could've won contests in. Her partner Lucas was travelling to see his family in another state for New Year's Eve. Ainsley had cut off their family because of bullying, abuse, and constant misgendering.

Ash herded everyone into the dining room and they all introduced themselves as they took their seats around the table. Fern had set the places out beautifully, complete with crackers waiting to be popped. The two friends brought plates of food from the kitchen and placed them in the middle of the table, ready for everyone to dig in.

'Oh no.' Bethany was staring at her phone with troubled eyes. 'My friend Sarah just had a huge fight with her parents. Her dad found out she's trans and kicked her out. I'm sorry, I think I might have to go.'

'Invite her,' Ash said without hesitation.

'Are you sure?'

'Absolutely. That's what this is for. Anyone who needs a family or a place to go. Invite her. Hell, she can stay in my spare room if she needs it.'

Bethany thanked him and headed out to pick up her friend.

Fern headed back outside, and this time everyone joined him while they waited for the girls to get back. Family dinner was for when the whole family was there.

***

Bethany returned twenty minutes later, followed nervously by a girl with short brown hair. Ash could sense her unease. He knew what that felt like and wondered how he could make it right.

'Hey, I'm Ash. Thanks for joining us, it's great to meet you,' he said with a warm smile.

'Hi. Are you sure it's okay for me to be here?' she replied quietly. Her voice was soft and sad.

'Absolutely. In fact, I'm glad you're here.' He paused again. 'What are you into? Do you have any hobbies?'

She perked up a little. 'Yeah, actually. I'm an artist. Or, I'd like to be. I love to make things. Mostly for my friends.'

'Oh my gosh. I have the perfect gift for you,' he cried, running off into the loungeroom. He returned a moment later, carrying a single present wrapped in Christmas paper in one hand, and dragging a tub of smaller gifts behind him with the other. He handed the large one to Sarah and called out for everyone to head back to the dining room.

'I know I don't know you, but I wanted to make sure everyone here was still able to enjoy Christmas this year, and not feel alone,' he said once everyone was seated again. 'We may not know each other, but we're family now. A wise man once said "Family don't end in blood", and sitting here, in this group of people disconnected from the blood that should've held us, we've created our own family. A family we can be more proud of than anything blood has given us. A family of outcasts.

'And while it's not the most important thing, gifts are a big part of this day for a lot of people, and I wanted to make sure no one was missing out on any of the special experiences, like the opportunity to tear through wrapping paper and find out what's inside. I don't know what you like, but I hope, if nothing else, you at least have fun opening a gift. Thank you all so much for joining us here.' Ash smiled. He dug into the tub of presents and handed one out to everyone to rip into before they ate. The group opened their gifts, excitement and laughter breaking out over the room as they discovered the things hidden inside. Ash watched Sarah quietly pull open the paper covering the craft kit and her eyes immediately lit up.

'I love it,' she whispered, tears filling up her eyes. 'Thank you. It's perfect.'

Fern smiled at Ash from across the table. 'Let's make this the best Christmas ever.'

The Pit

Darkness had fallen, and so had he.

Yet, unlike darkness, he did not stop, nor did he switch back to his former state. He hadn't just *fallen*, he was *falling*. The feeling was endless and he could not stop. He didn't know where he had fallen from, and there was no sign of where he was falling to. There was no visible ending, or even a beginning, only darkness. Occasionally there would be a flash of light. It would spark up suddenly in a way that reminded him of the flash on a camera, but the light would always leave as soon as it had come.

During the long periods of darkness, his eyes would eventually begin to adjust and he could start to make out what appeared to be shadows chasing each other in the distance. Were they chasing each other, or were they after him? He tried to follow them sometimes, see where they were going. He tried to see if they were moving towards him or away from him, but he never could. Sometimes it would feel as though he had almost got it worked out and then suddenly it was darker again and once more he felt blind, as though someone had closed the curtains in an already dark room.

He reached out repeatedly into the darkness, hoping for a hand to hold that could stop him from falling, or a branch, just anything to hold onto. There were moments when he could sense something, feel something close by, but it was always just out of reach.

Sometimes it felt as if he was falling faster, though he knew it wasn't possible to fall faster than the general pull of gravity that was constantly weighing him down. Then there were times when it felt as if everything had slowed down. He couldn't decide what was worse: simply knowing that you're stuck falling forever, or doing it in slow motion.

The strangest thing about him wasn't that he stayed persistent for as long as he did. No, the strangest thing about him was that he knew he was falling, he knew there would have to be some kind of end, some kind of bottom to this pit, he knew there was an end and he didn't know what it held, but even knowing all that he knew, he still wasn't afraid. In fact, he found the darkness comforting.

At least the darkness, he thought, *was predictable.*

It carried on like this for quite some time. Darkness, movement, flashes of light, the brush of something there but never more than a brush or sense of presence.

But then the noises came.

When they began, they were quiet and slow, like distant echoes crawling through the air and tangling themselves in his mind. Soft, but harrowing. Then, gradually, they got louder. Closer. Harsher. They were much more distinct now, like the desperate cries of a cat lost in the depths of night, combined with the fierce growl of a carnivorous beast, hungry after being trapped in starvation. Suddenly the neutrality he had felt before was rapidly dissipating, and it became incredibly clear to him that whatever consistency the pit had seemed to hold was limited and bound to shift at any given moment.

He thought of his mother, so young and full of life, ripped away by a disease she lacked the tools to fight.

He thought of his childhood dog, Sir Scraggles, playing joyfully and going a step too far.

He thought of his favourite series, something many would dismiss but holding significant space in his heart, cancelled, never to reach its well-deserved conclusion.

He thought of his best friend, the final words they shared, entirely unaware they would be the last when he left their favourite meeting spot, never to return again.

Everything good in life would soon be torn away, abrupt and unexplained, never the same again. The only true constant was the loss of good things. Life had proven this to him in countless moments over the years. It was time for him to finally accept it.

As he continued to fall, the noises got louder. They were all he could hear now, violent and cruel, crushing him and filing into the depths of his mind. His chest felt heavy, his lungs burned, and the darkness somehow felt darker than it had before. He couldn't breathe. Was he drowning? The air had turned thick in his throat and gripped tight from the inside, pulling all the pieces of him closer together. Implosion was only a single wrong breath away.

But he had already given up.

Somewhere along the way, as he fell through darkness upon darkness, loss upon loss, and the pain stacked up so high he could no longer build enough steps to see over it, he had reached his final conclusion. He didn't care anymore. He couldn't, he didn't have the strength to. So when the monsters came, their claws reaching out through the darkness, their breath heavy and humid against his skin, he made no attempt to fight back.

They came so suddenly, searing pain covering his body almost instantly as they tore into him, hissing and snarling as they rearranged every inch of his flesh. Pieces that were here were soon there, and pieces that were there were nowhere at all. Maniacal screams forced their way out of his throat as the monsters ripped him apart with violent and jagged teeth and claws.

There wasn't much left for him to hold on to. The years had taken every last scrap of hope, shattered it, and trampled it in the dirt, leaving only dust in place of the very force that should have kept him alive.

And now they had him.

Trapped.

Nowhere left to run, and nothing left to lose.

And he felt himself

slowly

falling

a p a r t

and then there was the light.

He couldn't see anything, only the bright white light that filled his vision.

Was it light? Or was it simply a different form of nothingness?

He couldn't feel anything anymore. Not the monsters, not the pain, not even the sadness that had weighed so heavily on his chest for so many years. He was no longer constantly aware of his body, his physical existence. Nothing felt *there* to him.

Except *she* was there. He could see her now, walking towards him from the bright white nothingness, with a brown furry mass plodding along beside her, his shaggy hair bouncing with every step. She waved and called out to him in a voice he hadn't heard in years. He waved back and she smiled. She'd always had the most beautiful smile. Another form appeared behind her, a young man with a crooked grin and sad eyes. He, too, waved.

Stopping only metres away, as if they hadn't been so distant only a second earlier. They greeted him as if nothing had changed, as if only hours or days had passed since they last spoke, and a warm feeling flowed through him that could only have been described as *home*.

And he knew everything would be okay now.

All of the darkness was gone, and with it went the memories, the pain, the loss of hope.

The darkness came, and it reached out and latched on to everything it could find, and then it went away, taking everything it had touched away with it, leaving him here, with his mother, his dog, and his best friend.

Everything was going to be perfectly okay, and nothing bad would ever find him here.

Never again.

D(ist)ress

The silence washed over him like a thousand insects crawling over his skin. Something was wrong, and it was choking him, gripping his throat as though someone had placed a vice between his shoulders.

The paper had piled up around him and from the moment he had felt the material touch his hands the dread had hit him like a crushing blow because he just *knew*, and when he took a deep breath and opened his eyes they only confirmed his fears. He scrambled through his brain, desperately seeking the words to explain what he was feeling as he looked down at the heap of fabric that had piled up in his lap. Soft, flowery, bright, and swishy.

Dresses. Several of them. As though someone had been searching for a way to disguise the words "*fuck you*" and throw them in his face.

Perhaps he was being a little harsh. Maybe he had been mistaken and opened the wrong gift. Maybe they had been meant for his cousin, all sparkles and sweet thoughts. Maybe she had good intentions, she hadn't meant anything by it, no foul wishes. But he had to say *something*. He had waited too long already and they were watching him. Waiting. He had to do something, he had to *speak*.

'Thank you, grandma. They're very... colourful,' he said, his voice straining as he struggled to force the words out of his throat.

'Oh, I'm so pleased you like them, dear.' Her smile grew until he was sure her face was about to split in two and her mouth would birth her skull. 'I picked them out especially for you when your mother and I went shopping together. The butterfly one was my favourite. I saw them and I thought "what would be more fitting than some beautiful dresses for my beautiful granddaughter?" and so I just had to get them.'

It took an astounding amount of energy for him not to wince. He had to remain polite, but it wasn't like she didn't know what she was doing. She knew, and she was damn proud of herself despite knowing.

'Well, sweetie,' his mum piped up. 'Which one's your favourite? How about you go put one of them on? It might do you good to change out of those daggy old shorts.'

He frowned slightly, barely managing to refrain from pointing out that he'd only gotten them a week earlier, and that, at her request that he leave one pair to be worn Christmas day, this was the first time he'd had them on. Instead, he collected the pile from his lap and headed down the hallway.

In his room, he took a closer look at the dresses. There were four of them, and they flowed so softly, so gently, almost as if they knew and were mocking him. *Join the club*, he thought. He spread the dresses across his bed and allowed his fingers to brush over them, feeling each one and how they would taunt his skin. One was white with multicoloured pinstripes, one was blue and covered in sparkly flower patterns, one was pale yellow with an orange fade on the lower half of the skirt, and the last one was shades of purple with embroidered butterflies. His grandmother might have been wrong about a lot of things, but he could at least agree with her that the butterfly dress was the nicest.

He changed quickly, keeping his eyes closed as he swapped out his t-shirt for the dress. Knowing he'd get in trouble if they could see them underneath, he also replaced his knee-length shorts with his school P.E. shorts. It was a small act, but it made him feel a little more comfortable. Wearing shorts under dresses made them feel less like dresses, and more like he was wearing an oversized t-shirt.

A *very* oversized t-shirt.

He sighed, messed up his hair again, and returned to the loungeroom where everyone had finished opening gifts and were now sitting around chatting.

Heads turned as he walked in, smiles spread on faces, and his mother gasped.

'Oh, darling! You look so gorgeous,' she exclaimed and waved her husband over. 'Look at her, isn't she pretty? How did we raise such a beautiful girl?'

Frustration boiled up inside him, bubbling over in his stomach, his mind, his lungs, trapping him underwater so he felt like he was drowning. His hand curled into a fist at his side, hidden from view in the folds of the skirt, nails digging into the palm of his hand in an effort to remain visibly calm.

'I knew they'd suit you,' his grandmother spoke, eyes sparkling in delight. 'What a lovely young lady you're growing to be.'

'You're wrong,' he muttered.

'What was that?' a voice said, he wasn't sure whose. His heart was pounding fiercely in his ears, his lungs were tight with dust.

'I said you're wrong. They don't suit me, and I'm not, as you put it, a lovely young lady. I'm not a lady at all.'

'Nicole, don't be so rude,' his mother snapped.

'Oh, she's just being silly. Kids always get a bit overwhelmed at Christmas. Especially the sensitive ones. She's just a girl, she'll grow out of it in a few years. Wait another year or so, when puberty really hits and the boys start chasing her.' His grandmother chuckled.

Puberty. The word punched him firmly in the chest and knocked the air out of him, taking with it the last of his composure. They'd started talking about it at school earlier in the year and he'd been forced into the group with the girls and it didn't make sense, *it didn't make sense*, it didn't. Make. Sense.

'I'm *not* a girl, and I'm not going to just grow out of it. Stop telling me I'll grow out of it! Stop telling everyone it's fine, that I'm just rude and sensitive and that *I'm going to grow out of it.* Just *STOP!*' he screamed, hands pulling at his hair, tears streaming down his face as violently as the rain had fallen from the sky on the day he met Laura.

Laura.

He had to see Laura.

He turned and ran out of the room, away from their sarcastic stares and teasing smiles and their awful, cruel words. In his bedroom, he typed a quick message to Laura, changed back into a t-shirt, threw on some jeans and sneakers, and shoved the dresses into his backpack along with a packet of biscuits from his hidden snack drawer. Laughter flooded the hallway and seeped under his door and he despised it, not their happiness, but the way they always seemed so much happier without him and his *drama*, his *complications*.

On his way out, sneaky as he thought he was, he ran into his uncle in the hallway.

'Where are you off to?'

He paused, cheeks still soaked from his tears, and looked up. 'I was just... going to check the mail.'

'Bullshit,' his uncle smirked. 'I get it, you need some space. They can be a lot sometimes. Heck, if I could duck out for an hour I would too, but I've gotta keep an eye on the kids so the missus can get caught up in her gossip squad. I'm not gonna tell on ya for sneaking out. Just be safe, yeah?'

Nicholas felt the weight slip from his shoulders and responded with a small smile.

His uncle's face slipped. 'Hey, you doing okay, kiddo?'

'It's fine. I'm used to it.' His heart fluttered at his uncle's question. Grownups didn't often ask if he was okay, at least not in a way that was genuine. 'I'm just going to meet my friend for a bit. I'll be back later.'

'No worries. You look after yourself. I'm here if you need anything, alright?'

'Alright.' He smiled and opened the door.

'And Nick,' his uncle called out. 'I'm sorry. You shouldn't be used to it, they shouldn't treat you like that. It won't always be like this.' He sighed and glanced over at the room down the hall. 'Try and be back in time for dessert. I'll see you later.'

***

He looked around at the empty playground, deserted while everyone spent time with their families for Christmas as he sat in silence on a swing away from the rest. Dumping his bag at the corner post, he began to swing, feeling the breeze against his skin and in his hair. The moments he spent on the swing were always the most magical; he always felt safe there.

Laura showed up a few minutes later, looking almost as miserable as he had felt when he'd arrived. She dropped her bag, a cross-body satchel, and took residence in the other swing.

Neither of them spoke for a while.

'I wasn't sure you'd come,' Nicholas whispered.

'Yeah,' she sighed. 'I slipped away when they were arguing.'

'Oh.'

They continued to swing.

'I wanted to wear a dress to dinner. Mum was okay with it, she's been getting better lately, sort of coming around and starting to accept that this isn't going to just disappear, but dad...' She started to cry.

Nicholas couldn't bear to see Laura cry. He thought back to when they'd met, years ago, and it had been him crying in the park. She had all but collected his tears and sent them back to the sky, leaving only sparkling trails of hope in their place upon his cheeks.

He jumped off the swing, setting a perfect landing, and Laura cheered as he took a bow before running to his backpack.

'Look, I want to show you something.'

She brought her swing to a stop and crouched beside him on the bark.

'So, my grandmother gave me these dresses and I... well, I kind of freaked out a bit,' he said, pulling them carefully out of the bag, making sure none of the fabric got caught on the zip. 'But then I thought, well, maybe they weren't actually for me.'

Laura frowned and tilted her head.

'I think you should have them. They're so beautiful and perfect, and they really are lovely dresses, but they're not... they're not for me. And you, well... they really couldn't suit anyone better. So, I'd like you to take them. If you want.'

'Nicholas, I don't know what to say,' her voice cracked as her eyes filled with tears.

'I'm sorry. I mean, you don't have to. Of course. I just thought that maybe you would like them, and they, and you, would both maybe have a better chance together.'

He looked up right as she leaned over, wrapping her arms around him.

'Thank you,' she whispered in his ear.

He passed her the dresses and watched as her eyes lit up and her smile grew with each one, the butterfly one clearly her favourite as well. She looked around quickly before grabbing the dress and running over to the tower and heading underneath, inside the space containing the fun mirror. A moment later, she emerged, fluttering purple flowing around her. She ran across and dumped her old clothes on her bag, twirling towards the open section in front of the swings and beginning to spin around and around, faster and faster. Nicholas grinned as he watched her, the dress blowing wildly in the air, and Laura, so happy and free, the happiest he'd ever seen her, twirling ecstatically until she could twirl no more.

'Thank you. This means the absolute world to me, Nicholas. Truly, thank you.' She smiled as though the world might end if she stopped and they took up their places on the swings once more.

The two of them remained at the park a little longer, Nicholas in his shorts, and Laura in her butterfly dress, and they knew it wouldn't be this hard forever.

They would go back home soon, but for now, they swung. Together.

And that was enough.

Project Milton

Dear Cody Phillips,

We are writing to inform you that you have been chosen as a winner of the Return to Life Project contest. Your essay on your beloved cat, Milton, swept the judges away with its passion, reasoning, and extensive research. The board was especially impressed with your writing, and your commitment to such a unique case, one that many would overlook.

We are absolutely thrilled to offer you the opportunity to bring Milton back to life as part of our program. Please fill out and return the attached form, and ensure you read the accompanying Terms and Conditions sheet.

Please note that if you accept this offer, you will also be expected to report and provide feedback on your experience in the following months. Also, note that this offer expires in a week. If we do not hear from you in that time, the offer will be passed on to the next most suitable candidate.

Regards,
Patrick Hutchence
Director, Return to Life Project

Cody read the email, and then he reread it twice to be sure he hadn't made a mistake. He did it. He got accepted. Only five people across the world would get chosen for this project, and he was one of them. Taking a deep breath, he tried to contain his excitement, but it was too much. It overpowered him and he let out a squeal of excitement as tears poured down his cheeks, running into his wide, toothy grin. When the project was first announced, he almost couldn't believe it. They'd found a way to bring people back. Something he had always secretly hoped for but never believed would actually be possible. He picked up his phone, typing out error-riddled messages to the group chat with his closest friends, careful not to let it slip from his shivering hands.

Tranwreck (Cody): I gto sccectped!

Tranwreck (Cody): They lied my essy

Tranwreck (Cody): oh my gosh *cries*

Piesexual (Allie): You what? Slow down. Try again.

Tranwreck (Cody): They LIKED my ESSAY. I got accepted! Return to Life accepted me! I'm getting my baby back! I'm getting Milton back!

Piesexual (Allie): HOLY CRAP! CONGRATS!! I'M SO EXCITED FOR YOU!!!

rainbowcrash (Lou): Yesssss!

Samberlin (Samuel): wait, what's happening?

Piesexual (Allie): Dammit Sam

Samberlin (Samuel): oh, that's amazing! proud of you codes! can't wait to finally meet him!

Cody didn't waste any time on his response. As soon as the group chat had been informed, he pulled up the attached documents, read through the terms and conditions, and filled out the form. He checked over both thoroughly, ensuring he hadn't missed any key details, and sent it off. His body relaxed as he let out a sigh of relief.

'And now we wait,' he whispered.

***

'He hates me,' Cody whimpered.

'He doesn't hate you. He's probably just going through some adjustments.' Allie had come over to keep him company, but they'd also said they thought he might need some support. They'd come equipped with a bag of Temptations cat treats, and a packet of Sour Patch Kids human treats. 'How long ago did he die? Ten years? A lot has changed in that time.'

Cody had always felt excited and independent in his first unit. He'd been living in the same place for a few years, and he'd never regretted it. Not once. Until now. How could he do this? How could he grow up? And change? And leave his childhood home? How dare he age and morph into something unrecognisable from the person he was ten years prior!

'I was seventeen when he died. And I hadn't been out that long. Or... well, I'd been out a couple of years, but not enough to change anything. I wasn't on T then. What if he doesn't recognise me? What if it's my fault because I transitioned?'

'It's not your fault. Transitioning was not a mistake for you on any level. Maybe he just needs to get used to the environment he's in, but he *will* figure it out. Give him some time.'

The two of them sat together on Cody's bedroom floor. Milton was hiding under the bed, where he'd been since his arrival. There was a saucer on the floor between them, freshly filled with Whiskas biscuits.

'I just really wanted you to meet him. He was already gone when we met and you never got the chance to see how beautiful he was.'

'I will, just not right now. Maybe we should leave him alone for a bit, give him some space. It's probably intimidating enough being in a new situation, let alone being cornered by two people and having to go between them to get food. Plus, we've got no clue what he's been through or what he's feeling. Y'know, with the whole being dead thing,' Allie said softly. 'We can come back and check on him later. Maybe he'll come out if he feels less trapped.'

Cody didn't speak, he simply stood up in response, and they left the room. He knew they were right, but it still tore holes in his chest and made it harder and harder to breathe. They were right that Milton might need some space, but what if he never got comfortable? He couldn't let that thought slip from his mind. Instead, it latched on and clung to him, sending prickles into his skin.

While he'd waited for Milton's arrival, Cody had done everything he could think of to make sure the house was ready for him. There was a corner in the bedroom with all of his old toys, his scratching post (previously torn to shreds, but recently fixed into a useable condition), and his special blanket. A shelf in the cupboard had been stocked with cat food, both wet and dry, and a bag of treats. He'd even spread out the old dressing gown Milton had always loved so much, never missing an opportunity to curl up for a nap whenever it was left out too long.

He could only wait and hope it would be enough.

***

'I don't understand why you chose Milton,' Cody's mum said, disgust clinging to the edges of her words. 'He's just a cat. You could've brought back anyone. Why not Grandma Rosie? Everyone loved her.'

'Because Milton is important to me.' He gasped, immediately recognising his mistake. 'Grandma Rosie didn't even like me that much. And besides, she'd lived a long and full life.'

'But she could have had another chance with this. She was a human being, Milton is a *cat*, Cody. A freaking cat. He might be important to you, but what about everyone else?'

'It's not about everyone else. I wrote the essay about the most important person in the world to me, I couldn't just choose someone else to bring back when I got the chance. That wouldn't be right.'

'They should've disqualified you for that.'

'Well, yeah. That's why I didn't. I wrote my essay on Milton, so he's who I chose,' he said, frowning as he spoke.

'No.' His mum laughed with exasperation. 'I mean they should have disqualified you for writing about your cat. The subject was "the person most important to me". Not cat, *person*.'

He ran his hands through his hair and latched on at the back, something he did when his stress levels were getting too high.

'Look. Milton was the most important person to me. Maybe he's not an actual person, but he was the most important *to me*. Not Grandma Rosie, not anyone else, Milton. As I said before, Grandma Rosie barely liked me. Why would I choose her?'

'Just because she didn't start calling you Cody or changing how she spoke about you doesn't mean she didn't like you. It's been years, get over it.'

Her tone had switched to something more vicious with her final sentence. Had she been given the ability, she would have spit venom.

'If you care about someone, you tend to be supportive, you don't do things that actively hurt them. She couldn't even manage the bare minimum for me. That's not caring. I gave her so many chances, Mum. She made that decision, not me.'

'They're just words, Cody,' she sighed. 'Not knives.'

Cody smirked. 'They might as well have been.' He walked to the front door and opened it carefully, hoping she'd take the hint. When she didn't, he simply stated that he'd like her to leave, he wanted to be alone.

After she left, he went to check on Milton again, taking him a dish of wet food and the bag of treats, just in case. Sitting on the floor in the middle of the room, facing the bed, he placed the dish on the floor and nudged it closer towards the bed, away from him. He waited a few minutes, took a treat out of the bag, held it out to him, and shook the packet gently while reaching out and rolling the treat between his fingers. Cody had often been able to lure Milton somewhere with this trick, even when there wasn't actually a treat there, somehow even just the illusion that he was rolling something was enough to get him running across the room.

But not this time.

Milton didn't run.

Milton stayed under the bed, hiding and out of sight.

Cody grabbed Milton's blanket and spread it out on the floor next to the bed and patted it a few times.

'Come on, Milton. You love this blanket. It's *your* blanket.'

Milton stayed put, darting green eyes staring out from underneath the bed.

Cody left him alone again to give him another shot with space.

***

Later that afternoon he headed back to the bedroom and turned just in time to see the flicker of a cat dashing back under the bed. The dish of wet food had been licked near clean, and the blanket was warm and slightly scrunched as if someone had been sleeping and left in a hurry. A grin stretched across his face and he ducked down and tried calling out to his cat, who was once more tucked up in the corner under the bed, staring out.

'Miiilton, kitty kitty kitty! Puss puss puss! Pu-uss!' he called in a sing-song voice. 'Miiilton, kitty kitty kitty! Puss puss! Come on puss puss!'

But Milton still wouldn't come out from beneath the bed.

***

It was all futile. Cody had tried everything. His favourite food, his toys, blankets, everything he used to love, and Milton wasn't responding to any of it. Two days later, repeating the same steps, racking his brain to think of anything else he could do to inspire safety and comfort. He felt hopeless. His heart had been grasped by a fist of devastation that only ever pressed further closed. He couldn't take it any more and he was close to giving up completely. This cat had broken his heart once before, digging his claws into Cody's very soul and tearing through it as he slipped away to the afterlife. It had very nearly destroyed him the first time, he wouldn't last a second time.

He sank down on the couch in the lounge, elbows on his knees, head in his hands, tears streaming gently down his face. The tears turned quickly into great, wrenching sobs, fingers in his hair clenched and pulling, folding in on himself and resisting the urge to scream.

Instead, between sniffs, he began to sing.

He sang the first line, each word cracking in his voice. Three more lines as he fought the tears trying to break through. Something shifted in the corner of his vision, startling him. Milton was carefully making his way down the hallway. Cody used to sing this song to him all the time. Whenever Milton had been upset or grumpy or just wouldn't let anyone near him, Cody would start singing this song, and it relaxed him. Milton would go from hissing and swatting to happy and purring, from rejecting the slightest boop to welcoming a pat and a hug. He sat up and wiped his face before continuing with the next verse. The cat had made it to the doorway now, watching him curiously as he kept singing, making it most of the way to the chorus before Milton cut him off.

A soft white paw touched his knee with caution, followed quickly by the rest of the cat, all black and brown and magnificent. He let out a soft meow as Cody let out his own similar sound, crying again, but no longer from the touch of a broken heart. This time he cried out of love, and relief that he'd finally done it. After ten long, agonising years, he finally had his cat back.

Milton stood on Cody's lap, reaching a paw over each shoulder and resting his head against his neck. Cody hugged him back, tightly but delicately, and he swore that this time he would never let go.

'I love you, Milton, more than anything, and I'd do anything for you. I'm so sorry for how it all ended, I'm sorry I couldn't help and that we didn't realise something was wrong sooner. But we're together again, and that's all that matters. I'll never let anything happen to you again, and I'll never let you go. Thank you for all that you've done for me.'

Milton hugged him tighter as if to say '*I know. I forgive you. I love you too.*'

Bad Parenting

Is it the fear that rests in the hearts of others, or the fear that rests within our own that pushes us to move along?

***

The Sunday afternoon air was warm and still, the only sounds were those of children playing in the distance, and the tapping of my fingers against the keyboard as I moved around an artificial world. Sunlight poured down over the freshly mowed lawn outside my window. Everything felt quiet and at peace, as though nothing could disturb the moment.

Then my phone rang, shattering the illusion as a Bon Jovi song filled the air, creating something far less than peace. Groaning, I reached over to pick it up.

Six months. I haven't heard from her in six months. Why now?

'Hello.'

'Hey munchkin, it's mum,' creaked the voice from the other end.

I said nothing, waiting for her to explain her reason for contacting me so suddenly. It was too late into the year for Mother's Day, far too late for her birthday, and an equal distance to Christmas.

'Ya there?' she screeched.

'Yeah. Why are you calling?'

'I'm gettin' married.'

'Oh. Really?' My tone was neutral, but verging on disbelief. It wasn't the first time I'd heard this. Hell, it wasn't the first time I'd heard it in the last twelve months. I wondered how long she'd known this particular partner, and how long it would last.

'Yeah. I want ya to meet him. Are ya free on Tuesday for dinner at the sports club?'

'Uh, I guess,' I responded hesitantly. I hadn't heard from her in months, and all of a sudden she wanted to meet, as though nothing had happened.

'Cool. So meet me at eleven at the plaza and we'll go from there.'

I paused, stunned in disbelief. Surely I hadn't heard that right.

'What? I'm not meeting you in the morning for dinner. I'll meet you there. What time?'

She stuttered slightly before telling me to meet her at six, a slight unease dripping from her voice.

I ended the call and stared at the phone on my desk, shaking my head. *There's no way this is going to be good.*

She'd always been like this, always disappearing for months on end only to show up and expect things like nothing had happened. Every time I'd end up thinking it was the last time, that she wasn't coming back again, and every time she'd show up out of nowhere and let me down all over again.

My phone pinged again, this time with a message from my best friend, sparking an idea like a match in my head. We'd only known each other for a few months, but we'd grown so close in that time and got along better than any friends I'd had before. Billie and I had met at a protest for queer rights and by the end of the evening we were cracking jokes and sticking rub-on tattoos on each other's faces (or, at least, I was cracking jokes while xe stuck a rub-on tattoo on my face). Xe had a bag in a black, grey, purple, and white pattern, which I'd immediately recognised as being the asexual pride flag colours, and xe got excited that someone had *finally* got it for once. Now it was uncommon to find a day where we weren't hanging out, or at least texting memes back and forth.

Jonah: Hey, you free Tuesday night?

Billie: Perhaps. Might I ask why?

Jonah: My mother wants to meet for dinner.

Jonah: [voice message]

Jonah: That was too much to type, sorry

Billie: Hold on a sec.

Billie: That's so weird. She just called you out of nowhere?

Jonah: Yep. I've never even heard of this guy before but now they're getting married and she wants me to meet him.

Billie: So are you going?

Jonah: I told her I would. Wanna come with me? We can meet up early and walk together. Dad's got a meeting.

***

When Tuesday arrived, I was more than a little nervous. Pins bounced around in my stomach like a bingo ball dispenser. I hadn't seen my mother in almost seven months, and I had no idea where she'd been or what she'd been doing during that time. She'd texted me last December and that was the last I'd heard.

After one final check on Google to make sure I knew which way we had to walk, I said goodbye to my dad, telling him I'd let him know when we were done so he could pick me up from Billie's after his meeting, and headed off.

Billie and I met at the plaza and walked along the old highway. Xe wouldn't remember when it was the main road before the freeway was put in. Xe lived out of town until a few years ago when xer dad got a new job and the two of them moved here. We filled the silence of the walk singing Queen songs and talking about the most ridiculous things we'd seen on Twitter so far that week. It was five minutes to six when my phone rang, churning out that all too familiar Bon Jovi song. I stopped to answer the call and Billie took the opportunity to touch up xer eye-shadow lipstick.

'Hello?'

'Where are ya?' her voice pierced through the phone.

'A block away. We said six, I'll be there by then.'

She grunted some mumble of a response that vaguely resembled 'I'll see you in a few minutes' and hung up.

'Was that her?' Billie asked, tucking xer makeup back into xer bag.

'Yep,' I sighed. 'We're not even late. It's five to and we're only a block away. We'll probably get there exactly on time. I don't know what her issue is. It was weird enough that she wanted me to meet her in the morning for dinner, but calling to ask where I am when I'm not even late? So weird.'

'Yeah, that is weird. And you hadn't heard from her for a while, had you? She just suddenly invited you here?'

'Well, yes. But that's happened before. She does that. She'll disappear for a while, then show up demanding we see her more. Y'know, as if she wasn't the one to drop contact in the first place.'

I could see her standing on the street outside the pub, facing the street we were walking down, looking around anxiously. We came to a stop on the footpath as she approached us. Something flickered on her face as she looked at me, her focus appearing forced and direct.

'Hi,' I said.

'Yeah, hi. Ya comin' in?' she cawed in response, starting to turn with the expectation we would follow.

'Hi, I'm Billie.' Billie spoke confidently and with a smile, xer voice clear and careful as xe introduced xemself as my mother grunted, no longer able to pretend xe weren't there, and struggled harder to hold back a look of... discomfort? Annoyance, perhaps?

'Rebecca. How do ya know *Jonah*?' Where Billie's had resembled kindness and life, my mum only added darkness to an empty night sky. Her voice dripped with poison as she spoke my name, grating it across her tongue like it was the most disgusting word she'd ever taken a moment to taste.

'Oh, I'm his friend.'

'Right.' She stared at us for a moment and took off towards the entrance.

We followed closely through the car park around the side of the building, coming to an abrupt stop a few metres away from the main door. My mother, now properly visible in the light from the overheads surrounding the building, was looking worse than when I'd last seen her. Her hair had thinned out, barely clinging to life across her scalp, and skin had tightened over her face leaving dips in her cheeks, and the pits around her eyes were so deep and dark they looked permanently bruised. Skeletal, almost. What once were bright blue orbs now stared out in a dull grey. A voice that many years ago could have whispered sweet lullabies now returned only the sounds of scraping gravel on pavement.

She took a few steps closer to the door and immediately backtracked, stopping to look around again, going back and forth between seeming as though she might go in, and pausing to glance around. Her motions were glitchy and uneven, like an NPC in a lagging video game. This cycle only lasted a couple of minutes, but the cold air and the uncertainty of what was happening dragged it out.

Finally, the action finished loading, and she lurched right up to the door before stopping again and turning to us.

'Ya both got ID?' she asked, as the sound of a metal shovel sliding on concrete escaped her mouth.

'Uh, I actually didn't bring my wallet,' Billie said. 'I didn't think about needing ID.'

'I don't have mine either. I took it out of my wallet for something the other day and forgot to put it back in,' I added.

'Well, ya can't drink without it,' my mother snarled.

'We don't drink anyway, so we shouldn't need it.'

'Oh. That's great,' she added, staring at me for a second while the shadow of a thoughtful look lingered on her face. 'Wait here a minute.'

As she took off inside, passing the reception desk and heading into the restaurant beyond, Billie and I looked at each other, eyes wide and speechless from what was happening.

'Why would it even matter? I honestly didn't even think about needing ID, I usually just carry my card with me.'

'It doesn't. We don't need ID to eat, and we're only here for dinner. I don't know what she's doing,' I mumbled on the off-chance someone else was around to hear us. With the way my mother had been acting, it seemed quite possible she was waiting on someone else to arrive. 'It's creeping me out a bit, actually. Like, I know she's always been a bit off her shit, but she's being incredibly weird tonight.'

'Oh. She's not normally like this?'

'Nope. This is a bit *extra* off. She's not usually so... jittery.'

'Hm. Yeah, it is a little creepy,' Billie agreed.

The doors opened again, right on cue, but instead of stepping out, she'd stopped to talk to the receptionist and somehow persuaded the young brunette to follow her out.

'She said ya can come in, but ya can't drink.'

'Yeah,' the receptionist continued. 'You're allowed inside, but you can't drink, and you can't go into the room where the pokies are. You don't need ID to have dinner.' She gave us a warm smile and headed back to her counter, free of the chilling breeze and the hollowness of Rebecca's stare.

Billie and I started to head in, but my mother wasn't following. Instead, she tottered further away again and started digging through her purse and checking her phone with fingers that seemed barely able to hold it.

'This isn't gonna work. We'll have to go somewhere else.' She twitched as she spoke, and her voice flickered with distortion between words.

'Okay,' I said slowly as we approached her. 'Where else do you want to go?'

'Dunno. What other pubs are there?'

I glanced at Billie with a frown. Why was she asking this? She lives here, she's been to all of them. Heck, she probably knows about more than I do. I'd never been to this one before tonight. There was no reason why she'd need to be asking us what was around. And yet...

'Uh, well there's The Walla?' I suggested. The Wallaby Hotel, but locals called it The Walla. It was a bit bogan, and there was almost always a fight breaking out, but it was probably the closest.

'Can't go there.'

'Okay. Uh, the other one that's across the road from The Walla. Near the five-way intersection. What's that called?'

'Eh, not that one.'

'Okay, well... I don't know.'

'What about Summerdale Tavern?' she suggested after a pause.

'Okay, uh, is that alright for you, Billie?' Even though she'd asked for suggestions, she'd been so quick to turn down everything I'd come up with. Still, if she'd thought of one that suited her, it could work.

'Sure. That works.'

'Yeah, cool,' my mother muttered. 'Well, my boyfriend can drive us there.'

I hesitated. We still hadn't even met this guy. We hadn't seen him, or even a sign of him, for that matter. How did she expect us to just get in a car with a complete stranger? Especially when I hadn't heard from her in so long.

'Or we could get a taxi and meet you there,' I suggested.

Her face scrunched up as she contemplated the idea, something harsher than darkness staggered behind her eyes threatening to take over. 'Nah, actually, it'll be fine. We'll stay here,' she said, taking off back towards the building. But she stopped. Again. She stopped just short of the entrance, looked around a few times, and then looked straight at me. The darkness, empty and alive, seemed to stare with her. 'Y'know what, I don't even wanna be here. I didn't wanna come. It wasn't even my idea, it was his idea. I didn't wanna see ya or contact ya, but he pushed me to and talked me into it. I didn't even wanna come.'

'Okay,' I blinked.

'Yeah, so I'm gonna go. I didn't even wanna be here.' We watched her as she took a few steps before turning back. 'Actually, here. Here's twenty bucks. Get a taxi home.' She shoved a twenty dollar note into my hand and took off across the car park.

All I could do was stare in the direction she'd headed until she'd made it completely out of sight. I hadn't expected this to go brilliantly, but I certainly hadn't expected... that, whatever it was. Silence suddenly fell over us like a sheet as we stood watching in slight shock.

'I, uh... I think maybe we should wait a few minutes. Just in case. It's pretty well-lit here. We'll just give it a few minutes and then head back,' I suggested with a shaky breath. Billie agreed, and I sent my dad a quick message to let him know we were heading back to Billie's.

The darkness that surrounded us no longer felt comforting. It no longer wrapped around us like a blanket of safety. Instead, it loomed, like a creature that could only be fuelled by threats to safety, and stolen breath. It clawed at our skin and exhaled bad dreams on our necks as we trudged back along the unlit streets that lined the way between trepidation and safety. It wasn't a long walk, just over ten minutes, but by the time we'd made it back to the main street, we were coated head to toe in the grime of anxiety. The sickly lighting of the service station called out to us like a warm hug; calm and inviting.

'Maybe we should stop for a few minutes.'

'Sounds good. I'm not sure I'm ready to go back to an empty house just yet.'

'We also still haven't eaten. Sorry about that. I honestly had no idea it would be that bad,' I said softly. 'But it's kind of wild how I'd made that joke about taking you to foil any plans to kidnap me or whatever, and then she was acting *so* sus. Like, you being there genuinely threw her off and she was so weird about it.'

'Yeah. Maybe she really did have a plan.'

'Well. Her level of agitation did seem to increase when we said we didn't have ID, too. Which is just... why would that matter? I don't get it. We came for dinner, and we *do not* need ID for that. I did actually have mine, by the way, but the way she reacted... I can't even begin to understand what her issue was.'

We headed in, bought a couple of potato cakes and a drink each, and sat down at one of the tables to calm down and recover some energy. The discomfort between us was heavy and thick but was quickly dissolved with a few jokes and some hot potato. It wasn't long before we'd finished eating and felt ready enough to finish the journey home, but as I began to stand I caught a glimpse of something through the shop window.

'Holy shit,' I whispered, sitting back down.

Billie looked at me, a slight frown lingering on xer face. 'What?'

'She's out there.'

'She's *what*? Where?'

'Far side, near the car wash. Same way we came.'

'What? Why? Should we go?'

'I don't know. She might not know we're here, but I don't really want to find out. I... I don't think she'd be following us, but after everything else tonight, I don't really know what to expect. I definitely don't want her to know where you live,' I stuttered. 'But if we stay in here a bit longer, at least it's got light and people. Plus, she seemed desperate to get away from us before, maybe she'll just leave when she realises we're here.'

I watched discreetly as she trundled across the property, past the petrol pumps, and in through the doors. She looked as though she was making a conscious effort to look anywhere but the tables where we sat. It took her several attempts to pick up an item from the snack display near the front counter as the ability to grip evaded her. When she reached the register, too far behind me to watch without raising suspicion, I turned my gaze to the screen above the coffee machine to keep an eye on her through the active security footage while she paid. On the screen she was blurry, appearing slightly darker than the rest of the image, and looking more like a blob of thick mist than the solid being she was. I kept my eyes on her as she left, stumbling back in the direction she'd come from. Neither of us spoke for a few minutes as we continued to watch, waiting to make sure she was really gone. I'm not sure how much time passed.

Three minutes.

Thirty.

It was almost seven thirty by the time we left the protective borders of the service station, heading quickly and quietly the rest of the way home, and looking over our shoulders every couple of metres just to be sure we weren't being followed.

We made it back to the house in record time despite our overlapping fixation on safety and the hope we held in finding it back at home. But that dream didn't last. It couldn't. The illusion cracked like glass all around us as we crept through the gate and a feeling hit with a crushing blow to tell us *this wasn't right*.

The air felt wrong, somehow, like it had been taken out of being and replaced with something far more sinister.

The moon took cover in the clouds in a final move to ensure we were alone in the world.

The silence mocked us.

Billie rushed for the keys to let us in, but xe were too late. She was already there, waiting for us. I felt the air rush out of my lungs and they struggled to find enough to refill as I watched her approach from the doorway, feet several inches from the ground. Her eyes were rolled back and blood ran down her face, dripping carelessly on a pale dress. A cracking like footsteps on twigs rang out across the yard, my mother's floating body contorting effortlessly into what should have been an unnatural shape, promptly followed by a piercing scream.

The ground around our feet cracked and split open, forming chasms and cutting us off from the outside world. What once held an assortment of plant life now played host to growing flames. My mother cracked again, hands tearing desperately at her eyes.

And my hands tore at mine.

Hollow screams form inside my chest and erupted from the tangled creature's throat. My skin began to tear as I picked it apart, ripping and clawing my way through, squinting through bloodied vision as the being that was once my mother became less and less.

The fear that rested in my heart pounded with encouragement as it came to life, growing and swirling in the darkness, lifting me up, and burrowing into the pile of flesh and screams in front of me. I continued to dig; my hands and body a grated mess, hers now a hollowed-out cage. Her fear, barely visible now, remained only as the remnants of ash on the floor of what had once formed a person. She hadn't been human in a long time. Fear had been given too much freedom, and it had taken over. Eating away, consuming her until there was nothing left but an echo of who she once was, and leading her further and further away from herself until she could truly confront the source.

Something far bigger and darker than she could even begin to imagine.

And even then, after everything she'd done and the trouble she'd caused, while I lay bloodied and bruised, watching coloured lights reflect in flickering patterns on the wall as I drifted out of consciousness, I still found myself wishing her well.

Good Friends

Her words bounced around in his chest like bullets, ricocheting off every surface, leaving holes in the comfort of *never having to deal with this*. His heart felt wrong. Someone somewhere had mixed up the pieces when they were building him and it was something that could never be fixed.

A girl liked him.

She actually *liked* him.

And all he could do was rummage around through the skip bin of thoughts that disguised itself as his brain and hope, *hope*, that maybe there would be an answer floating around in there somewhere.

I have a crush on you, and I'd like to go on a date with you one day.

He felt sick.

Was that how it was supposed to feel when someone liked you? Not exciting, or happy, or curious, but *sick*?

He felt ridiculous for taking too long to say anything back, scared that if he did he'd have to actually see it through, and ashamed because he wasn't even sure what he could say in the first place. What if he said the wrong thing? Upsetting her was high on his list of things he definitely *did not* want to do, but unease snuck into his veins and whispered that it would happen either way.

'It's okay, Aiden. It's fine if you don't want to,' she rushed. 'I probably shouldn't have said anything.'

'No, I... It just caught me off guard a little, that's all.'

'That's okay. We can think about it. Maybe one day.' She turned back to her game, filling the screen before her with flashes of bullets and blood. A girl made of fairy floss and clouds finding comfort in the loudness of violence and brutality.

Her smile was gentle and his breath caught in his lungs.

He cursed himself for being broken.

***

His best friend, Cayda, stared at him, their smirk cutting through the stillness in the air. He'd just told them about Imogen, and how he'd likely screwed up their entire friendship, and they seemed... amused.

'Oh my gosh! I thought it looked like you two were getting along pretty well. How did you respond?'

'I didn't, really. Honestly, she told me, and I just felt sick. I completely froze up.'

'Ooh, so are you going to ask her out?' they asked with raised eyebrows, as if they hadn't heard what he'd said at all.

'I-I don't know. I'm not sure how to respond. The whole thing was just really confusing.'

'Why was it confusing? Do you like her?'

'I don't know.'

'What do you mean you don't know? How do you feel when you're with her?'

'I mean, I... she's nice?'

'Do you get butterflies?'

'Sometimes. I haven't seen as many lately though. Maybe it's the weather? I've seen quite a few dragonflies though. But I'm not sure what that has to do with Imogen.'

'I meant butterflies in your stomach,' they laughed.

'That doesn't even make sense.' He frowned, unsure what they were finding so amusing. This conversation was infuriating; it was like prickles in his chest, not so much that it was overloading him at once, but enough that it would build up over time. A small sensation, just out of his reach. 'She's nice, I enjoy hanging out with her, we have fun, we get along really well…'

'So, what's the problem?'

'She said she has a crush on me and wants to date.' The words felt awkward in his mouth, like instead of speaking he'd been chewing on a cushion. His body felt tight and his face felt warm and he wished so desperately that he could evaporate into the air where no one could find him, no one could see how out of place he looked with his friends who all knew what they wanted, and no one could interrogate him on his confusing feelings and make him feel like an idiot for not understanding.

'You're blushing,' Cayda sang. 'You do! You like her!'

'I don't know. I don't know if I do, it's just confusing. I think we're just good friends.'

'Aiden, your face is bright red.'

'No, it's not.' He shrugged his shoulders as if they had a chance at hiding him. It was so embarrassing, not knowing how he felt and having to listen to his friends telling him. How could they know his feelings when he wasn't even sure himself? And why was it so easy for them to figure it out when they couldn't feel what he felt?

'You can't hide, I saw it. You have a crush on her too, you should ask her out!'

'I don't know…'

'She likes you, she said so herself, right? She *wants* to go on a date with you. And you like her. Ask her!'

'But what if I don't like her? I think we're just friends. Like, good friends.'

Cayda groaned in frustration. 'How does she make you feel?'

He thought for a moment, trying to picture what things were like when they were together. 'Calm, I guess. Safe. Fuzzy? I'm not sure how to explain it, really. I feel like things can't be bad when I'm with her. Kind of like I'm covered in an incredibly soft blanket.'

'Crush. Case closed. Do it.' They turned and headed into the kitchen, giving their words an extra sense of finality. It should have been a relief to have the answers handed to him in such a direct way, so why did it feel more like a sentence? He'd never been good with crushes or dating, and he often found himself struggling to identify his feelings. Maybe Cayda was right. They had a lot more experience than him, after all.

***

The following evening he waited at the bus stop in the town square. After his conversation with Cayda, he'd messaged Imogen and the two of them had arranged to go for dinner. He'd suggested they should meet at the bus stop so they could choose where to go together. His bus was ten minutes earlier than hers, and even though he was in the middle of a really good book on his phone, he couldn't focus. Instead, he paced back and forth, flicking his fingers as if they could shoo away his nerves.

A bus pulled up and his heart froze in his chest. He felt like he was going to be sick. Everything was too heavy, it was too much, why did he think this was a good idea? Why did he listen to Cayda? Why did he-

The bus pulled away. His body relaxed, softening from stone to something a little more solid than jelly. It wasn't hers. Not yet. Cayda had assured him these feelings were only nerves, but this didn't feel like nerves to him. It felt like something else, something more like... fear? He wasn't afraid of Imogen.

He continued to pace and flick, keeping himself calm until Imogen's bus pulled up. She stepped out the back door, pulling her headphones down around her neck, eyes lighting up when she saw him, enthusiasm fuelling her pace. Imogen was wearing a pale pink dress with sparkly leaves embroidered in a darker pink, light glittery makeup, and a pair of purple converse. She looked beautiful, and Aiden felt proud when he saw her. Not enamoured or fluttery, but proud.

'Hey,' she called out cheerfully, stopping directly in front of him.

'Hey. Uh, do you have any preferences for where we should go? What's your food tolerance like today?'

'Low.' Nothing too intense, no heavy flavours, and definitely no new food.

'So, somewhere with chips then?'

Imogen nodded.

'How about that place on the corner two blocks down? The one that used to be the Italian restaurant with the catchy ad that now haunts our dreams fifteen years later. I think it's a bit of a hybrid place now. They do a little bit of everything. Pizza, pasta, stir fry, parmy, and chips, of course. Some other stuff too, probably. I don't know. But they have a few options, and they definitely have chips if you wanna check it out?' He was rambling. Gosh, why was he *like this*? Shut up, shut up, *shut up*.

She agreed with a soft smile and grabbed his hand to hold as they walked, a habit they'd picked up a few months earlier, for both comfort and the reassurance they wouldn't find themselves separated. It was funny, he thought, how her reaction to stressful situations was to shut down, resulting in mute episodes, but his response was the opposite. When he was overwhelmed he couldn't *stop* talking, no matter how much he wished he could. The more he rambled the more stressed he got, and with every word, it became harder to stop.

When they arrived at the restaurant, Aiden headed to the counter and ordered for them while Imogen found a booth in the far corner in hopes that it might be just the slightest bit quieter there. Even if it wasn't, at least they would be more comfortable there than at a table, and they wouldn't be surrounded. That was something they had in common, at least. He paid, thanking the attendant, and carefully carried the drinks to the table, placing a coke down on the table for Imogen, and a raspberry soft drink for himself.

'They, uh, didn't have any straws,' he mumbled apologetically.

'That's okay.' She smiled. 'I have a pack in my bag just in case.' She pulled one out and placed it in her own glass before offering him the pack. He did think it was incredible how organised she was. It was one of the things he liked most about her and one of the reasons why he never felt like he had to worry about not being prepared for situations when he was with her. Where his brain felt scattered, like an office left open in a storm, hers was a fully labelled filing cabinet.

It didn't take long before he began to spiral, recognising the silence that had flicked on between them, and realising he had no idea how to go about conversations on a date. Were they different to the conversations they would normally have? Were there certain rules he had to follow in this context? He made a mental note to ask Cayda at a later point, but for now, he was stuck. Conversations weren't something that typically flowed well between them anyway, they were often short-lived spurts of interaction based around something one of them had done or seen and wanted to share or a quick little *"I miss you"* text when the break between words had gone on a little too long. But this felt worse. There was this pressure to talk about *something*, but it had to be the right kind of thing. Something appropriate for... a date.

'How... was... your day?' he asked, his voice peaking at the end, lingering with uncertainty.

'Oh! I took some photos a few days ago, I think I showed you. But I spent today editing them,' she rushed. 'I don't know if you remember the one I took of Cayda's cat, but I took that and edited the cat's face into another photo of the sky to look like Mufasa. I forgot to have lunch and didn't realise until like the middle of the afternoon, but it was really cool.' Her eyes lit up as she spoke, making him smile. She was really into photography and had done some incredible work with it. So much time and passion went into each individual piece. He really hoped she would stick with it and pursue it.

'That sounds incredible. I'd love to see it sometime.'

Before she could respond, a server arrived at the table, placing a bowl of chips in front of Imogen, and a bowl of napolitana pasta for Aiden. He sighed in relief with the understanding that conversation was no longer an expectation while they could focus on their meals. The food before them decreased, eating in near silence, serenaded by the shouts and cackling laughter from the tables surrounding them as the number of guests rapidly grew in time for the dinner rush. Imogen was starting to fidget, tapping rapidly on the table, anxiety building up due to the new sensory input.

'We can leave if you want,' Aiden offered. 'It's getting pretty crowded and loud in here.'

Imogen nodded, shrinking into herself a little. He helped her wrap up the rest of her chips in a napkin and placed himself like a barrier to protect her from potential collisions. Once they'd made it out, she relaxed, letting out a sigh of relief as she smiled and took his hand. Her thumb drew swirls on the back of his hand and she stared across at him in adoration. Fear lit a match beneath the skin of his cheeks and his stomach grew a fist that reached up to grip his chest, tightening around his heart and lungs until he no longer understood how to breathe. Imogen, oblivious to his hesitation and unease, leaned in until their faces were close enough to touch. She gently pressed her lips against his, damp and wriggly. He wanted the earth to swallow him whole. Luckily, it was also brief. He tensed his body in an effort not to pull a face when she stepped back, eyes still shining up at him.

'Well,' he sighed. 'That was-'

'Aiden!' someone called out, saving him from finishing the thought. Marco, an old classmate from his high school, was walking towards them. 'Hey, man! I haven't seen you in ages. How've you been?

'Uhh, alright. What's, uh... what's going on?' Anything to avoid the current *situation*. He and Marco had never really been close. They hung out during lunch breaks, but never anything outside of school. In fact, Aiden was a little shocked he'd approached them at all.

'Not much, my man. You folks doin' alright? Everything good? All swell?'

'Yeah, we're okay. We just got dinner and it was getting a bit crowded so we... oh, this is Imogen. She's my, uh, friend. She's studying photography and does some really cool stuff with it.'

'Right on, right on. Listen, mate. I'll leave you to it. Hit me up on Facey later though, yeah? Alright. I'll see you later, man. Have a good one,' he said, raising his eyebrows to give Aiden a serious look before patting him on the back and heading back the way he'd come from.

Neither of them knew what to say as they headed back to the bus stop. Cayda didn't try to hold his hand this time, preoccupied with the squishy toy she'd been fidgeting with since Marco's interruption. They waited quietly for the last bus of the evening, and with a quick hug goodbye, they both headed home.

***

By the time he got home, he was exhausted. He felt unclean, the feeling growing stronger as discomfort crawled all over him and settled down inside his throat. They were having such a good time, why did she have to *kiss him*?

A bubbly notification sound shook him out of his thoughts.

> **Cayda:** Hey! How was the date? Im said it went well ;)

So, she'd told Cayda about the kiss. Realising this was not the distraction he'd been hoping for, he sighed, abandoning his phone on the front table to seek out a shower and fresh clothes.

And to brush his goddamn teeth.

He had a quick shower, hoping the soap and water would clean more than the physical ick from his body, that it could somehow reach inside his memory and wash away the feelings left behind. Afterwards, he retreated to the couch to watch TV. He needed something mindless and comforting after... all of that.

Halfway through the episode, his phone went off again. He frowned as he opened the message he definitely wasn't expecting to receive.

Marco: hey man, just checking you're alright. You made it home?

Aiden: Yeah. I'm just watching The X-Files. I'm okay.

Marco: you sure bud? You looked pretty uncomfy when I saw you with that girl earlier. Called her your friend. Looked a bit more than that. Hope I wasn't interrupting a breakup or anything

Aiden: Oh, haha. No. Uhh, it's complicated.

Marco: hit me with it. Only if you want to, but maybe I can help

Aiden: Well… it was a date. Kinda.

Marco: how is something "kinda" a date?

Aiden: She… I'm not even sure if I like her. We usually get along fine, but it all just felt so awkward and… weird.

Marco: if you don't know if you like her, why were you on a date?

Aiden: My friend Cayda told me to go out with her. Imogen told me she likes me and wanted to go on a date, and I told Cayda I didn't know if I liked Imogen, but Cayda insisted that I do like her even though… I'm really not sure I do.

Aiden: She's my friend, and I care about her a lot, but I don't feel any desire to date her. Cayda was so sure about it though.

Marco: y'know, it doesn't matter how Cayda feels. It's all you, man. If you liked this girl, you would know. It was shitty of anyone to push you into that. How do YOU feel about it?

Aiden: I… I've only had a crush on someone twice before, years ago, and it didn't feel like this. This feels like a close friend.

Marco: then tell them that. Don't let them push you into crap that doesn't feel right for you. Especially if it makes you that uncomfortable.

Aiden: She doesn't make me uncomfortable. She's my friend.

Marco: I saw that kiss, man.

Marco: hey, listen. Do you wanna grab coffee with me tomorrow? Have a bit of a chat? No pressure, obvs.

Aiden: Yeah. Okay, sure. That sounds good.

He usually felt nervous after agreeing to meet with someone, but, so far, the conversation had made him feel a little lighter. Maybe this would be good for him. Marco seemed like a pretty decent guy. Heck, maybe he'd even found a new friend. Chuckling to himself, smiling a genuine smile for the first time that day, he felt grateful that at least *something* good had come out of this disaster of a date.

***

Marco was already in line to order at the cafe when Aiden arrived. He paid for their drinks and a couple of fresh cookies, pointing to the table he'd already picked out.

'Thanks for meeting up, man,' Marco said with a smile.

'Thanks for the hot chocolate,' Aiden replied. 'And for talking with me about this. I know we were never really that close in school, but I did enjoy hanging out with you.'

'Same, man. To be fair, I always wished I'd been better at keeping in touch. I kinda had a lot going on back then, and, honestly, I was a bit of a mess. You kept me sane in that place.'

'Really?'

'Yeah,' he chuckled. 'I got my shit together, but it did take a couple of years. Half-assed a few courses, finally found one I enjoyed, met some good people, finally figured out some shit about myself, and here I am, better than ever.'

'I'm glad to hear things got better.'

'Heck yeah, bro. So anyway, tell me about this girl. What happened?'

'Well, as I said, Imogen told me she wanted to go out. I wasn't sure, but Cayda made some assumptions about how I felt and pressured me to go out with her. Imogen and I... we're just friends. We're really good friends, but that's all. I don't want to be in a relationship, and I definitely don't want to kiss her.' Aiden paused to pull a face and take a sip of his drink to wash away the ghost of a bad taste from his mouth. 'Why do people *do* that?'

'Do what? Kiss?'

'Yeah. I just... I don't get it.'

'Because it's fun. For a lot of people, at least.'

'Wait, people actually *enjoy* that? I thought it was horrifying. It was so weird and uncomfortable, and I felt so gross when I got home. Like, I actually brushed my teeth and... Oh god, I really am broken.'

'Hey, wait.' Marco frowned. 'You are *not* broken. A lot of people do enjoy it, but not everyone does. Some people hate it.'

'Oh, really?' Aiden relaxed a little, shaking some of the weight off his shoulders and smiling slightly as he watched it hit the floor. 'That is reassuring. But it's not just the kissing. I don't want to do any of it. I don't even get crushes. There's so much pressure to grow up and be in a relationship but I don't *want* to be in a relationship. Like, at all.'

The two boys sat with their drinks for a moment, taking a breath. Aiden had shed the weight of the kiss, but there was still so much making their conversation heavy. He took a long sip and let the drink defrost the cold feeling that had settled inside him. All he had to do was grow up.

'Y'know... you could be asexual. Or aromantic, maybe. Or both,' Marco suggested.

'I could be *what*?'

'I was just thinking... if you don't like kissing, you don't wanna date anyone, you don't get crushes, or any of that stuff... maybe you're aro/ace. Someone who doesn't experience sexual or romantic attraction.'

'I'd never thought of that,' Aiden said softly.

'Pretty sure there's a spectrum or something, like different levels or types or some shit. But from what you've said, it sounds like you could fit into that.'

'I didn't know that was an option. Everyone's just always going on about how important it is to be with people in those ways, and making me feel like I had to just suck it up and go along with it. Like it was something I had to just do one day.'

'No way, man. If it's not you, it's not you. My ex was ace. It was something that fluctuated for him, so sometimes he'd be okay with it, but most of the time he was pretty grossed out. Kind of like you were about Imogen kissing you. It doesn't fluctuate for everyone though. That's just something you'll have to figure out.'

'I... don't know what to say. Thank you,' Aiden stammered. 'I've... never really been interested. The whole thought of it horrifies me. I'm sure it's not supposed to. I really thought I was just broken and I had to just get over it, but... I think you're right.'

He finished his hot chocolate and the cookie Marco had given him while they continued to talk about their favourite things and everything they'd been up to since they'd left school. All of the weight had fallen and scattered, and Aiden finally felt like he could breathe. No pieces were missing, and he was never broken. He was just Aiden. Aromantic, and possibly asexual, and definitely one hundred percent Aiden.

To the Ground

Today I went down to the river and realised all my dreams were dead.

The flowers were blooming, birds were singing, and the sun was shining high above the trees that swayed in a soft breeze and patchily sheltered me so the harsh rays couldn't touch my head.

I'd left my house in a quiet frenzy, anxiety gnawing at my bones.

I couldn't recall the last time I'd been outside. Was it a few days? A week? Maybe it was longer. Time doesn't feel real to me anymore. It hasn't for so long, I probably couldn't begin to understand what any of it meant before. Locked inside, shut away, hiding all alone.

The cool air hit my gentle cheeks and clawed at my skin with the cold.

So different from the warmth and safety of the four walls that usually contained me, but on I walked, silence looming alongside my shadow. It's a short walk from my house, just minutes down the road, and after all these hours I've never forgotten to hold my breath at the right places along the trail that leads me there. I often wonder if I'll remember these moments when my hair is faded, my skin loosens its grip, and I'm classified as old.

The footpath is aged and cracked, weeds forcing through as they take back what once was theirs.

When it ended I found myself forced onto uneven ground. Grass, at first, cushioned each footfall and reminded me of all I could have been and could ever aspire to become. Though it soon gave way to hard, uneven dirt, I am grateful for the moments I had between, however short they might have been. The cars rushed by, screaming for attention as they carried their soldiers through many, possibly hundreds of individual wars. I wondered if either of them, the cars or the people inside, would remember how they came to be, or if they would hollow their hearts in whichever ways best allowed them to forget. Would they forgive each wrong and replace each loss, or would they all greet the end with uncorrected affairs?

Brushing them out of my mind, I continued towards the river, trampling down the side of the road.

Careless footsteps made their way across even more careless surfaces. Dust gathered on the cuffs of my jeans, flicked up from the soles of my shoes, while my lungs littered a different kind of dust that couldn't be cleaned away. The quiet I had on my journey faded as I approached the meeting place for the local aquaphiles, complete with the sounds of splashing and laughter. Children chased each other in loops and squiggles, darting between and around the vehicles in the designated parking areas, while grown-ups and teens who'd abandoned such dreams unloaded cars for their lunches and swimming gear. Not a person in sight shed a tear. I made my way through all the chaos and sound, the thoughts in my head spinning faster around, I tried to forget all the lies I had found in every waking moment up to this point. My footsteps grew heavier, thick with the weight of so many broken promises. The heartless breeze called out to me as more pieces began to corrode.

My feet carried me through, well beyond where people came to live, and further away into the dark.

The trees grew tall, reaching up into the sky, their branches towering over the path. Leaves piled in crisp autumn corners, soggy with condensation left over from the moonlight's laugh. I marched on, barely present, hardly aware, and minimally conscious. When the last of the cheeky screams faded from my range of hearing, I became encumbered by every last drop of dread that had soaked through my body over the course of my twenty-something years. That dread proceeded to burrow inside me, right into the depths of everything I had ever been, and, in an effort to make enough space for it to rest, pushed out every last one of my fears. Dread festered inside, fear boiled on top, and I felt the pieces of me crumbling away. I left a breadcrumb trail behind me as I walked further along the path, but the breadcrumbs were memories of hope I'd found reasons to discard. They slipped through apathetic fingers without the slightest bruise; not a mark.

Wandering deeper into the surrounding bushland, listening to the sounds called out by the birds sitting in trees and soaring across the sky.

They called out to each other, their family, friends, enemies; an orchestral flurry that darted back and forth through the air. I wondered if the birds knew the damage of deceit. Three magpies crossed my path to play in the long grass that rested between the trees that divided this trail from the other. I stopped myself, despite my buzzing melancholia, to watch them sing so sweetly. I pondered the dreams of Aves, sheltered from the many burdens of our human existence only to be brought down in a second-hand effort inspired by selfishness. The cruel façade of innocence shifted again, disintegrating in the aftermath of the thought, leaving only an ache in my chest to remember it by.

The further I walked, the darker it grew, and the less of me there was left to find.

Having strayed from the man-made path and with it my sanity, I ambled my way into a clearing. A dull little patch, far from the light that fuelled the living. It was here that I finally let go, allowing myself to succumb to everything that fed the darkness in my mind, allowing it to bleed into every inch of me, and consume me in a way not too different to how the insects soon would. Back flat on the ground, dirt lingering under the tips of my fingernails while I stared up into the patchwork sea of browns and greens, the sun no longer visible through the thickness of the branches, just me. Alone. In the dark. A single physical form resting in the dream of a million shattered pieces and counting. No one would look for me here. No one would try. Beauty gave way to sorrow to make up for their lies. Now look at me, at what I've become. Just another pile of rotting flesh and bones with nothing to leave behind.

Consequences

The man lived alone, fuelled by self-righteousness and delusions. He spent his days watching the same shows on the TV and drinking beer, and every moment seemed to be in wait for someone foolish, or equally motivated to visit so he would have someone to talk to and indulge in his deception. Some of his friends shared his views; others were aware of his mistruths and took no interest in opposing them. He had two sons who had both long moved out and had families of their own, still popping in to visit on the way to work or during lunch breaks, but never to tell him he was wrong. Never to deny or doubt him.

None cared to speak against him or his actions. He was a man that could do no wrong and no amount of hateful comments or abuse by him could change that.

Or so he had believed.

***

One morning, seemingly no different from those that came before, he woke up damp. A smell not too different from rust filled the room. Shifting into a sitting position, he peeled his eyes open and looked around.

Dark red liquid dripped down the walls and soaked through his sheets. It wasn't sweat that had clung to him as the sun rose that morning, but blood.

A shiver sped through him as he threw the covers away from his body. He leaned over and pulled on his prosthetic leg, followed closely by a pair of khaki shorts, socks, and sneakers. He staggered out of his bedroom and into the hallway, the floor squelching beneath his feet. It was just as bad as the bedroom had been, if not worse. The ceiling dripped, the bookshelves lining the wall ran like waterfalls, the carpet was drenched, and even the light flickered red.

He was just tired. He hadn't woken up properly yet. That was all.

He shook his head, moving into the bathroom. As he pushed the door open, shock barreled through him. The walls were damp, with patches of black and green, the mirror was cracked and rusted around the edges, and the shower curtain, held by only half its usual number of rings, hung limply, torn almost beyond recognition. The man made his way to the sink, turned on the tap, and splashed the blackened water over his face.

A car roared into his driveway and came to a stop. He closed his eyes and wiped the water from his face, opening his eyes again as the towel passed over his chin.

He blinked, rubbed his hand across his forehead, and turned slowly as his gaze made its way around the room. The carpet was dry and green, the shower curtain intact, and the water clear. He frowned and headed out to greet his visitor, shaking his head as he walked through the door connecting the hallway to the kitchen.

He was just tired.

His son stopped outside the back door, waiting to be let in for his usual visit on the way to work. The man decided not to mention the strange way he'd woken up that morning. He unlocked the door and headed back into the kitchen to boil the kettle.

***

Evening came around with no further incidents, solidifying the man's previous conclusion that his mind had been playing tricks in the midst of his exhaustion. He'd had a late night, after all, having stayed up later than usual to watch an old British investigator show he hadn't seen in years after stumbling across it on a new streaming app.

His friends had all come and gone throughout the afternoon, the last having just left. He'd just cracked open his seventh beer when a loud crashing sound came from inside the house, startling him, and causing him to spill his drink. Muttering profanities as he attempted to soak up what he could of the wasted beverage and standing the mostly-full bottle on the side table, he stumbled in through the back door and headed to the kitchen to investigate the source of the crash that had made him jump so.

When he saw that the kitchen was as he'd left it, he shook his head and continued to the bedroom to change into a dry shirt. Maybe he'd been distracted by the dampness of the t-shirt clinging to his skin, or perhaps he simply hadn't noticed the squelching carpet beneath his feet as he made his way down the hallway, but he stopped abruptly at the doorway to the bedroom, something prickling along his skin and whispering that something was off. He took a step back, looking down at the water flowing under the bathroom door and burst in, slamming the door open against the side of the shower. Water was rushing out of the shower, pooling in the bath below and spilling over the edge. The carpet was lifting at the edges, the entire floor was a puddle, and he cursed whoever had thought carpet had been a sensible option for a bathroom.

Careful not to slip, he reached into the shower to turn off the taps, but they were already tight. Frowning, he wiggled the tap again, the force shaking the wall of the cubicle. He stood up again, muttering and swearing under his breath as he threw the towels off the rails and onto the floor, charging through the door to pull what he could from the linen cupboard in the hall outside, and proceeding to throw them across the floor and pile them where the worst of the water had accumulated. Once he'd thrown down every towel he could find, he reach over to the tap once more, but as soon as his fingers brushed the edge of the metal knob, the water stopped.

Not so much as a drip followed.

Something must have worn through, he thought, deciding he'd take a proper look at it in the morning.

He quickly changed his shirt and headed back out to his seat on the verandah, picking up the empty beer bottle that had been abandoned on its side on the seat cushion, mopping up the rest of the wasted liquid more precious to him than life, and swapping the chair for a dry one. A fresh drink was plucked from the fridge and cracked open as he settled down to watch the news, the cool liquid making its way down his throat. Inside, like it should have been all along.

***

The following day he woke up as normal, no blood on the sheets, nothing dripping down the walls. Everything that had happened on Friday was a thing of the past, figments of his imagination brought on by an insufficient amount of sleep.

He turned on the television and stayed in bed long enough to watch the morning news before switching it off again and following through with his morning routine.

Attaching his leg, getting dressed, and going to the bathroom.

Being careful not to trip on the towels all over the floor, he bent down to pick a few up so he could hang them up to dry but paused when he felt the first one. It wasn't wet. He frowned and picked up another one, then checked a few more before sighing and throwing them back down in a heap. They were all dry. Not a single towel was the slightest bit damp. He ran a hand over his balding head and mumbled to himself before making his way to the kitchen.

Everything had been fine when he woke up, his bedroom, the hallway, and the bathroom were all fine. Clean. *Normal*.

But the kitchen was far from it.

Waves of shock tore through him as he ran his eyes around the room. Mould spread thick across the ceiling, the cupboard doors were faded and worn and barely hanging onto their hinges, the floor looked as though someone had tracked mud through, and the benches were coated in a layer of dust so thick it appeared as if they hadn't been touched in years. It looked significantly less like the house he'd lived in for almost forty years, and far more like one that had been abandoned as long.

The plan for a morning coffee was discarded as quickly as it had begun when he opened the fridge to fluffy vegetables, grey meat, and chunky yellowed milk. Though half of the food in his fridge had been well past its best already, mould creeping along the surfaces that he simply refused to notice, it certainly hadn't been this bad. So what if the cans in his cupboard had swollen from cylindrical to spherical? They were *his*, even if it wasn't something he'd ever eat himself, and there was no reason to throw any of it away.

Instead of a milkless coffee, he opted for making an attempt to clean some of the mess that had taken over his kitchen. This was where he cooked, where he made his breakfast, where he stored a hidden box of chocolate treats for his grandchildren, and he liked it to be perfectly immaculate. Not a spot on the bench, even when it was in use, and no hands but his own were to ever fix a meal in this space. Ever.

But here it was, falling apart and every inch covered in filth.

The man put his best cloth and spray to work, scrubbing at the bench, wiping down every inch, attacking every speck of muck. Every other room had built-up grime caking every surface, but not his kitchen. Never his kitchen.

He spent what felt like hours scrubbing and scraping, soaking and scrubbing again, but nothing seemed to work. No matter what he did, none of the filth would come clean.

By late morning he'd given up and surrendered to his old armchair to play card games on his laptop, allowing exhaustion to have its way with him as he fell into a snoring slumber.

***

A short while later, he woke with a jolt to the sound of the microwave going off, and a pounding in his head that echoed and throbbed with every beep that urged him to hurry over and end the incessant noise. Though he couldn't remember having placed anything in there in the first place. Had he simply forgotten and dozed off?

He pushed his TV table aside in a huff and plodded through to the kitchen (his beautiful, spotless kitchen) to where the microwave rested in a hutch above the sink. Unable to shake the peculiar feeling that something was off, he paused, turning his head around the room, taking in every detail. But everything was fine. There were no dirty dishes save for a single plate from last night's dinner, there hadn't been anything left on the benches, not a speck of dirt in sight.

The microwave beeped again and he muttered for patience under his breath before reaching up to poke the *open* button. The door sprung forwards, smashing into the wall and breaking the glass as dark red liquid gushed out. Blood poured furiously from the appliance, onto the bench below where it dribbled like a waterfall over the edge, splattering all over the floor. It erupted with the force of the wind in a storm, covering the man, and forcing him back to the other side of the room where he stood pressed against the opposite bench, watching his perfect kitchen turn red.

Disgust gnawed away at his insides, and horror clawed at his throat as he attempted to speak, but no words could be forced out that felt equal to what he had just witnessed. The blood had stopped pouring from the microwave, but the substance still coated everything in sight, the thick smell still lingered, and the sticky feeling that glued him in place made him feel as though he might never be clean again.

***

After washing the blood from his arms and face in the bathroom sink (due to the shower refusing to turn on at all) and changing into a clean set of clothes, he'd retreated to his usual seat outside and opened his first beer for the day. It was only one-thirty, but he'd earned it after the morning he'd had, and besides, *it's five o'clock somewhere.*

The first beer was the fastest, fuelled by a desperate need for the bitter drink to fill his stomach and the hole he felt without it. It wasn't a man and his beer, the drink was part of him; without it, he could never be complete.

That first bottle joined the rest of the empties in a box against the wall, and his hand found its way around beer number two. Fingers wrapped tightly around the neck of the bottle as he sipped the cold, bitter drink and it flowed through him as naturally as any bodily fluid. He continued on this way for quite a while, bottle after bottle down his throat and in the box, and time passed as if he existed as a separate event.

A familiar tune began to play nearby. At first, he'd assumed it was coming from the television, but the familiar voices of *Antiques Roadshow* continued to drone on as normal. He brushed it off, continuing to stare at the old British guy through the screen as he admired bowls, vases, and hair pieces, but the tune gradually got louder and harder to ignore. Picking up the remote and muting the TV, he looked around, trying to figure out where it was coming from.

With the TV silent, he recognised the song as the one he would often play on the drive home after winning a round of golf. It played softly, only recognisable by its distinctive tune.

Something inside smashed and the man jumped.

The song turned right up and blasted the final line of the chorus before switching off entirely.

He shot up out of his seat and stormed inside, through the laundry and into the adjoining granny flat. The door from the main house to the laundry slammed shut behind him, followed by the sound of a turning lock. He backtracked to the door, snatched the handle and shook it hard, but it was definitely locked.

The laundry itself was a mostly empty room with only a washer, dryer, and a small table. It had a windowless toilet on one side, a large window showing little more than the fence that separated his property from his neighbour on the opposite side, and a door at either end. The man did a quick check from where he stood, and once he was sure there wasn't anyone hiding to jump out at him, he headed through the door at the other end into a two-room granny flat, surfacing in the main room; a living space with a small kitchenette. This wasn't a part of the house he often went in; it was mostly used for storing things that were too good to keep in the shed and items that belonged to his sons that wouldn't fit in their own. The bedroom through in the back was empty except for an old couch section.

It used to be full of life...

but he tried not to think about that.

It didn't matter anyway. Not any more.

He pressed on through the room. Piles of camping gear were stacked in the corner, threatening to topple at any wrong touch. He couldn't say why the laundry door had locked behind him, but it would be easy to fix. He just had to head outside through the granny flat's main entrance, through the verandah, and back into the main house where he kept the key.

Simple fix, he thought.

But as he made his way across the room, the further he went, the more he realised something was wrong. The second door slid shut, cutting him off from the laundry, and the lights began to flicker, getting faster and faster

and faster

until they suddenly stopped.

And the man turned slowly, frowning as he looked around the near-empty room in the darkness because he couldn't fathom why everything had gone black when it was the middle of a rather sunny afternoon.

A shrill beeping sound filled the room, and he raced to cover his ears, causing him to drop his beer in the process, losing an extension of himself like another detached limb. The smell of burning toast wafted through the room in air so thick he almost could have bitten down.

When the lights flashed again, they illuminated a dark red stain across the back wall. The man took a few cautious steps closer to try and work out what it had been, and when he stood right before it, there was another flash.

HIS BLOOD IS ON YOUR HANDS

He took a sudden step back, glancing down at the hands that hung down, wet and dripping red. He tried to wipe them off on his jeans, but nothing seemed to make any difference to the soaked and stained extremities.

'*DO YOU HAVE A COCK?*' a voice boomed, loud and forceful, laced with aggression and hatred. The man didn't respond, but spun around, looking in every direction for the culprit. '*DO YOU HAVE COCK?*' it screamed again. The words were vile. Vulgar. Dripping with malice. He didn't want to listen to this. He didn't have to listen to this. Instead, he turned back towards the laundry, attempting to force the door open but failing as it refused to budge.

His only way out was the main door, back through the room and right up beside the bedroom door. If anyone was hiding, lurking, it would have to be in there.

No.

What was he doing? He wasn't afraid. Perhaps he'd fallen asleep again and this was all some absurd dream.

But as he walked over the worn-out carpet, forcefully but still shaking, it all started up again.

The voice.

The lights.

The feeling of dread burrowing deep inside the pit of his stomach in a way that suggested it had no intention of going away again.

'*DO YOU HAVE A COCK?*' the voice went on.

A flash of light struck the room and a flicker of a young man appeared in front of him. The outline of his late grandson, standing before him in front of the bedroom door, exactly where he'd stood when those same words had been directed at him from the man's own mouth all those months ago. Ghastly glowing eyes lit up the young man's face as a crooked grin stretched wide, ripping open the skin at either side as a hollow voice cried out and the grin uttered the words '*Do you?*'

The man stood facing the apparition, rolling it over in his mind like some sick joke. It wasn't his fault. None of this was his fault.

'*DO YOU HAVE A COCK?*'

Sure, he was protective of his kitchen. He had to ban the young man from cooking. That didn't mean it was his fault when the young man couldn't get access to food.

'*DO YOU HAVE A COCK? DO YOU?*'

Sure, he'd often say something had to be done a particular way. Sometimes those things changed and had to be done the opposite way. It wasn't his fault he'd get so worked up about the young man doing exactly what he'd been told to do because it wasn't right anymore. It just wasn't.

'*DO YOU HAVE A COCK?*'

Sure, he complained about water usage. There was nothing wrong with threatening to turn the water off if the young man tried to have a shower. That didn't make it his fault that the grandson he'd invited to stay was no longer able to have access to the shower.

'*DO YOU? DO YOU HAVE A COCK? DO YOU?*'

None of it was his fault. He'd only made the invitation in the first place. Maybe he'd put bans and restrictions on a few basic things the young man, like every human, needed to survive. He'd even made some easy money out of it while he yelled, threatened, called names... but it wasn't *his fault* that the young man had died after being kicked out with nowhere else to go. It hadn't been his hands that sculpted those final moments. That was all self-inflicted.

After all, he couldn't have done anything wrong.

He just wasn't that kind of person.

Not at all.

***

The man's son had worked from home on Monday because one of the kids had been sick. When he arrived on Tuesday morning for his usual coffee, the man wasn't waiting for him. Since the car was still in the driveway, his son let himself in with a spare key and put the kettle on, ensuring it would be ready when his father joined him. Sometimes the man was late out of bed, only surfacing when he heard the low rumble of a visitor pulling up.

But after a few minutes, when the coffee had been made and the man still hadn't appeared, his son went looking.

The old man was found sitting in his armchair.

Unmoving.

Unresponsive.

Covered in an assortment of bodily fluids as he stared straight ahead.

The paramedics came to pick him up and take him away. They'd guessed he'd been that way for at least a day, possibly two.

No one would ever know what had happened to the man during that time. Even if they did, they would never understand.

Then again, maybe there are some things better left unknown.

Breathe

When Nicholas saw the bag in his mum's hand as she came through the front door, his heart dropped like a plummeting guillotine, cutting off the air that usually filled his lungs. He'd known this was coming. It was something he'd been worried about for the last couple of years and something he'd been dreading for the last few months.

But she was so calm.

She didn't appear to have a single worry or concern as she called to him and began to pull the items of clothing from the bag. His new uniform for high school. A blue plaid dress, a pair of white socks with three rings around the top in the school colours, and a floor-length skirt for winter. Why didn't they understand this uniform wasn't made for him? Growing up should be for discovering yourself and finding things that bring you joy and make you feel good and alive, but as he got older all he was getting instead was a deeper hole in the pit of his stomach, forever burrowing deeper, forever growing darker.

His mum still hadn't accepted that he was trans, but at least she'd stopped deadnaming him. The word "Nicholas" had still never left her mouth though, and he found himself clinging to flickers of hope that floated alongside the ever-growing dust that one day, *one day*, she might finally get it.

But he wasn't going to push his luck.

'Here, Nicky, try these on,' she said, with the kind of smile she fed strangers on the street as a way of ensuring they knew her family was *perfect* and everything was *fine*.

Nicholas did as he was told. There was no energy to fight when that fight wouldn't achieve anything. There was certainly no energy to fight when all it would bring about was more screaming, his mother crying, his father yelling, and everyone hardly speaking for the next three days. Not over *a dress*. They didn't need a repeat of what had happened at Christmas a year earlier. He took the dress and tried it on, just to show his mother it fit, just to keep her happy. She looked at him with his overgrown hair and his wobbly smile and beamed like the sun outside had found a way through her face. Her happiness clawed at his skin while the uniform suffocated him and made everything feel wrong, wrong, *wrong* and he stood there and took it because it was a perfect fit and he had nothing to complain about.

He found he almost liked the winter uniform. *Almost*. At least he could wear pants underneath without anyone being able to tell him off. It didn't make him feel sick in the same way the summer uniform had. It was something to hold onto.

***

When the first day of school rolled around, his hair almost reached his shoulders, and his mother insisted on him wearing a headband to keep it tidy. He wasn't allowed to get it cut anymore; it had to meet the uniform guidelines. Girls, as he had been labelled, were not permitted to have hair shorter than their chin.

He got dressed slowly and with a heavy reluctance, all while his mother called to him to *hurry up or we'll be late*. The dress fell just above his knees, so he couldn't wear his usual shorts underneath without them sticking out the bottom, but his P.E. shorts were perfect. Still, he found himself longing for the uniform he'd worn for the past six years.

In primary school, everyone had looked the same, all dressed in navy blue shorts and a sky-blue polo shirt, but high school calls for segregation the same way baby birds cry for their parents. In high school, boys would wear grey shorts and white short-sleeved button-up shirts with a logo on the pocket, while girls would wear a dress in the school colours with a white collar. There were also different rules regarding every inch of your body, many of which were bordering on absurd.

His mother dropped him off at the gate, and he clambered out of the car, rushing over to the sign where he'd promised to meet up with Laura so they could head in together. They figured it would be easier, at least, if they didn't have to figure out everything alone.

'You're late,' she said sullenly. Her hair was combed back, her face scrubbed clean of any sign of life, and she frowned at her shoes as she pulled on her clothes. 'We'd better hurry up. Year six lockers are on the far side, over by the playground.'

Nicholas knew better than to ask if she was okay. He knew she wasn't. The best he could do was *be there* and support her, even if it meant he had no room left to be there for himself. She'd done so much for him, after all. At least he only had to wear these clothes for school, he could wear whatever he wanted at home, but Laura didn't get that same kind of freedom. This was the only time he had to wear something that didn't match how he felt. If he was feeling suffocated because he had to wear a dress for a few hours, he couldn't begin to imagine what it felt like for her.

They arrived at their building just in time for the bell, but the rest of the class was still standing around, chatting loudly, and showing off their favourite gadgets. A middle-aged man scurried out of the classroom with **A1** marked on the door, almost trapping the sleeve of his shirt in his haste. When clearing his throat didn't grab the attention of the group, he clapped in one of the many familiar patterns ingrained in kids since first grade, and the students clapped their return in a reflex that came as easily as breathing.

'Your lockers, are being upgraded,' he announced. 'They should have arrived last week, but due to the weather, there have been some delays. We are expecting them to arrive by the end of the week, but for now, you will leave them along the back wall of A1 or A2 depending on your class placement. Listen for your name, and *quietly* take a seat in your designated room.' He paused to wave at another teacher, a lady with short orange hair and bright swishy clothes. 'Ms Walsh, if you could.'

Ms Walsh read out the names of each of the forty-odd students gathered before her, glancing around to catch the face of each child as they headed towards their designated room. Nicholas heard his name and felt his chest grow tight. A1. He winced and glanced over at Laura. She returned the look with an apologetic smile.

He wanted to stay and wait.

He begged the universe to let him wait, to stay with Laura and see if they would be put together.

But when he didn't move, his name was called again and two sets of eyes, one soft and welcoming, the other harsh and demanding, settled on him.

'You, with the headband. It's okay, sweetie. You're in with Mr Hammond,' the kind teacher said, offering him a smile. She looked back at the list, running her finger down the page. 'Actually, the only person left in my room is Addison. Everyone else, head to A1.'

They spent the morning reading page after page of information; school rules, uniform regulations, the appropriate way to submit assignments, and everything else they'd heard before. Timetables were handed out along with their school diaries. The emergency procedures were rushed over in a way that made Nicholas sure he wouldn't have the slightest idea what to do if anything ever happened.

And finally, after an hour and a half of paperwork and information being dumped on them all at once, the bell rang. Mr Hammond dismissed them for lunch and reminded the class they were not to take their bags, only what they needed for lunch.

Nicholas and Laura were halfway through the door when their teacher called out for them to wait.

'Your hair is too long,' he said to Laura when he caught up to them. 'The dress code states that all boys should keep their hair tidy and of a respectable length.'

'I know it's gotten a bit messy. I'll make sure to keep it tidier tomorrow,' Laura responded softly.

'It's not just messy. It's too long. You need to get it cut. This is your first warning, you have until the end of the week. If it's still this length next Monday, you'll be getting detention,' he snapped.

'But I can make sure it's tidy. I can keep it neat. I can't cut it any shorter, please. It took so long for it to grow at all.'

'Boys shouldn't have long hair. The rules here are not that strict compared to other schools. Think yourself lucky you're not required to shave your head.' He stopped to pull a sheet of paper out of his binder and thrust it towards Laura. 'Here's the uniform code. Please familiarise yourself with it and ensure there are no further slip-ups.'

Laura nodded carefully, staring at the printed page in her hands, afraid to speak in case she resorted to tears.

Mr Hammond, seemingly satisfied and looking rather pleased with himself for managing to upset a student so early in the term, turned back into the classroom and closed the door behind him.

Nicholas carefully steered Laura away from the windows, adamant that he would not allow such a nasty man the satisfaction he seemed to crave. He would not let that man see his best friend cry.

The two friends sat together on the grass at the side of the building, leaning back against the cool wall. There was no need to speak; nothing they could say would change the moment for the better. Laura began to pull anxiously on her hair, barely reaching her chin on average, and a careful sob escaped her.

But before she could start properly crying, they were approached by an older student, marching confidently in odd shoes and dropping her pin-covered backpack in the dirt in front of them as she sat down.

'Mr Hammond's such a hard-ass, don't even worry about it,' she said, shooting them a friendly smile. 'I had him for year six as well, two years ago, and he's not had a good day in at least that long.'

Laura wiped her eyes with caution and offered a sad smile in reply.

'I'm Emery, by the way.'

'I'm Nicholas. This is Laura.'

'Hm, I thought that might be the case.'

'What?' asked Nicholas. He knew to be cautious with strangers, but he felt he could trust Emery. She reminded him of the first time he met Laura in the park when they were younger.

'Trans kiddos.' She smirked and dug around in her bag. 'The uniform rules are bullshit. They're definitely enforced, too, which sucks. Though they do seem to be picky about which kids get in trouble over it, and that is such an utter load of crap. Just a bunch of grown-ups with sticks in their asses looking for more ways to control everyone they view as less important,' she mumbled.

'But there are ways around them. You don't have to cut your hair, you just need to be clever about hiding it. Can I show you?'

Laura nodded and whispered 'Okay.'

Emery stopped digging and pulled out a small container of pins. She grabbed a couple and reached across to Laura, frowning in concentration as she placed pins in the younger girl's hair, moving them around until she was satisfied. When she was finished she sat back and pulled up the camera on her phone for a mirror.

'What do you think?'

Looking carefully at the phone, Laura tilted her head in every direction. She reached up and touched her hair, feeling the pins underneath the layers, but understanding they were not noticeable in a way that could get her in trouble.

'It's amazing. Thank you.'

'No problem at all. Keep the pins, I've got an abundance anyway, and you need them more.' She turned to Nicholas, sticking her hand back in her bag and pulling out a hair tie. 'Yours is easily fixed with a winding bun, though with how short it is at the moment, you might need a couple of pins too. Just bunch up your hair, and twist it, like this.' Emery pulled her own light brown hair out of the pigtails that had held it up and began to twist it all together at the back of her head. 'Then when it feels tight, carefully move your hand in and wrap it around itself. Yeah, just like that! And then grab a tie, and just pop that over it a couple of times to keep it together. Does it feel better?'

'Yeah,' Nicholas said, surprise flooding through his voice. 'It does. I still know it's there if I think about it, but I can't feel it and it's not touching my neck.'

Emery seemed satisfied with this response and shoved half a snack bar into her mouth. Nicholas and Laura took the opportunity to eat something themselves. When they only got two breaks during the six-hour school day, it was important to make sure they remembered to eat, hydrate, and do whatever else their bodies demanded. The two younger kids watched Emery as she did a quick scan of the area before pulling her phone out of her pocket and typing faster than they had ever dared to.

'How are you kids feeling about the uniforms?' she asked, still intently focused on her phone.

'I'm used to dressing like this,' Laura said. 'My parents aren't supportive at all, so shorts and shirts are my full-time wear. Obviously, I wish I had the choice, but it is what it is and it doesn't really bother me too much at this point. Nicholas though...'

'I feel like I'm suffocating.'

Emery blinked. 'Blunt, but definitely gets the point across. Okay, that's fine, we can work with that. How would your parents feel about you wearing shorts and a shirt?'

'Fine. That's what I wear at home, b-but the school,' he stuttered, 'they wouldn't let me wear the other uniform. They've got me listed as a girl and that's all they'll let me be.'

'Au contraire, young boy. Did you know the dress isn't the only option? There's a button-up shirt and shorts combo for the girls too, they just don't advertise it. Plus, the uniform shop lady is a major pain in the ass and will tell you the dress is the only option. You have to ask directly, and you have to be firm about it.'

Nicholas felt a weight ease off his chest, giving him permission to breathe again.

'It's not the same as the one Laura's wearing. The shirt is a thicker material, and the shorts are navy blue, so it's not as cool as the dress in a temperature context, but it's significantly less dress-shaped. And if your uniform is in good enough condition, which yours is since you've only worn it for one day, you can do a trade and pay the difference.'

'That... wow. That sounds amazing. My mum knows how much I hate them so I only usually have to wear dresses for really specific occasions, so I think she'd be fine with it. I'll check with her tonight.'

'Awesome sauce. I'll wait up near the front gate tomorrow morning so I can go with you if she agrees. Miss K knows me well enough at this point to know she can't get away with shit when I'm there, and I won't take no for an answer.'

By the time the bell rang, all three of them were laughing and joking with smiles reaching for their ears. Emery had a meeting to go to at recess, so they wouldn't see her then, but they felt much better knowing they had already made a friend. They had new ways to get around school rules and be who they were meant to be, and there was at least one person on their side, ready to help.

***

The following Monday came quickly and after two boring classes filled with excitement and fidgeting, Nicholas and Laura made their way back to the spot where they'd first met Emery. They'd agreed to get together every Monday for lunch, inviting any other queer students to join them, sitting in the same spot, catching up, and sharing handy tips they'd picked up that might help others.

First, it was just the three of them, but a couple of kids from Emery's grade soon joined in.

On the third week, Laura even brought along a notebook to jot down any info that seemed useful, as well as everyone's pronouns.

When other new students like them arrived, they knew what to do and how to help. Thanks to Emery, they were able to pass on the advice they'd been given. They would watch a scared face turn into one filled with hope and excitement, just as she'd done with them.

Week after week they would meet for lunch. Sometimes there would be a group of students all bunched together at the side of classroom A1, other times it was only the three of them. Sometimes they wouldn't talk about much at all, other times they'd be rushing to get the last of a story in before running to make it to class on time. Sometimes one of the kids would bring a hobby along and they'd all sit around reading comics or making matching beaded keychains.

On the days in between, Nicholas and Laura made their own group. They would, on the odd occasion, join in with other kids in their class, but most of the time it was just the two of them.

And, if they were being entirely honest, they rarely needed anything more.

Pirates

'Maybe we should be pirates,' Sky said, leaning back against an old tree beside the river. 'We could just sail away and take on anyone who tried to talk down to us.'

Andy looked at him, eyes sparkling at the thought of an adventure. 'Yes! Pirates live in a world free of discrimination, free from the confines of an ableist and homophobic society. We could be as queer as we like and nobody could tell us otherwise!' they cheered.

Sky's grin widened, taking over a good third of his face. He ripped open his tote bag, pulling out a pen and a notebook. 'Alright, I'm making a list!'

'Of course you are.' Andy chuckled at him, rolling his eyes.

The two boys began to think, shouting out all of the different things they might need. Food (something for every mood), water, spare clothes, blankets, emergency kits (first aid, and a repair kit), and a few tools. When they were sure they'd listed everything that they were most likely to need, Sky started a new page to divide up the tasks.

'We should bring Derek too,' Andy added. 'Every pirate crew could use a trusty familiar.'

'That's witches, bro.'

Andy frowned. 'Pirates have them too.'

'No, dude. Pirates have parrots.' Sky watched his brother's face drop. 'I'm not saying we can't take Derek. That's a great idea. The more the merrier, and I'd love to have him on board. We'll be breaking gender roles and companion roles all in one.'

Andy cheered and pulled himself up off the ground. 'Okay, give me my list. We can meet back here in an hour.'

'Better make it two,' Sky said, 'considering travel time, and the stuff we have to find.' He tore a page from the book and handed it to his brother. 'You're in charge of Derek, too. You just have to grab the emergency kits and your clothes. I've got a couple more things to get, but I think it'll even out with how long it takes to get Derek into the carrier.'

***

An hour and a half later, Sky was back at the river. He'd gathered everything on his list and had sat down to organise it all into piles while he waited for Andy to return. The food had been sorted between a tote bag and an esky to keep it fresh, he'd grabbed their dad's toolbox from the hallway cupboard, and he'd tucked his clothes along with a few blankets into a backpack.

They were totally set to become pirates!

Andy arrived twenty minutes late, lugging Derek's cat carrier, a backpack over one shoulder, and tugging a suitcase behind him. The wheels of the suitcase rattled against the dirt track, threatening to tip over at every slight bump or stone.

'Andy, m'dude, what is that?' Sky called out as he approached.

Andy frowned, tilted his head towards the cat carrier in his hand, and stopped in the middle of the track. 'Derek,' he said innocently. 'You said it would be good to bring him along.'

Sky rolled his eyes. *His fucking brother...*

'No, you idiot. Why do you have an entire suitcase? We're going to be pirates, we need stuff we can carry.'

'I can carry this. Look.' He continued to move forward, still dragging the case behind him.

'Carry. Lift. Pick up. You're dragging that.' Sky shook his head, running hands through his hair and flicking it off to the side. 'Did you at least get everything on your list?'

'Yes,' Andy whined. 'I got a first aid kit from the chemist, the repair kit Dad gave us when we moved, and some clothes.'

'The repair kit Dad gave us?' Sky asked, feeling his chest drop.

'Yes.'

'The one that was missing half the stuff?'

Andy was quiet, staring at something on the ground. 'Maybe.'

Sky let out an exasperated sigh and plonked down on the ground, spreading both legs out in front of him in a V shape, while Andy continued to stare at the ground, twisting his shoe in the dirt. Neither boy spoke, and after a few minutes, Andy kneeled down to check on Derek.

'I just don't know how you expect us to repair the boat with a half-assed repair kit,' Sky mumbled.

'What boat?' Andy looked up, frowning directly at his brother.

'The pirate boat. Duh.'

'But we don't have a boat.'

'Huh? What do you mean? We're gonna be pirates. Pirates live on a boat.'

'Dude. I know that.'

'Then what are you talking about?' Sky snapped.

'We do not have a boat. We do not own a boat. Neither of us brought a boat. So *what boat?*' Andy asked, waving his arms around, pointing at the river with a single occupied fishing boat. 'How are we gonna be pirates if we don't have a freaking boat?'

Sky's face froze for a moment as he looked around, finally picking up on what his brother had been trying, not so elegantly, to explain. His eyes dropped, his mouth slipping from his usual grin back to one of disappointment.

'Well,' he said. 'Maybe we need to put a little more thought into something like this. Being pirates isn't really something you can decide to do out of nowhere.'

'Oh,' Andy mumbled. 'Yeah. So... what are we going to do now?'

'I dunno. Head home, I guess.' Sky scrambled up from his position on the ground, dusted himself off, and picked up his bags, pausing for Andy to do the same.

The two boys trudged back up the road, away from the river, signs of a failed adventure filling every hand.

'Just because we can't be pirates today doesn't mean we can't try again some other time. There's always tomorrow!' Sky smiled at his brother and quickened his pace.

Andy continued to plod along, a suitcase trailing haphazardly behind him, and a cat carrier in his other hand, being careful to avoid even the slightest bumps for the sake of both himself and the cat.

'Or next week,' he muttered, forever cursed by his brother's excessive enthusiasm and complete disregard for common sense.

Sky, oblivious to his older brother's concern, continued to skip along.

'Yeah! How about Tuesday? That feels like the perfect day to become pirates.'

From Pianos to Petals

Brendon was a fine young man. His thick dark hair perfectly shaped his face, his sparkling blue eyes reflected every light, and his voice was as smooth as chocolate. On top of aesthetics, he was also the manager of a rather successful business. In many aspects, he was doing quite well for himself.

But his mother, while able to recognise his ability and good looks, was still not satisfied. Her son, as fond of him as she was, would never be truly successful until he'd found himself a bride. It was most important that he resolved this issue no later than his twenty-fifth birthday, as he would be getting older and less desirable.

Six months into his twenty-fourth year, she called him to request that he visit.

'You've got plenty of staff available to cover you for a few days,' she said. 'Take a week off and come up to stay. I'll be sure to cook all your favourite meals.'

After several minutes of nagging, he agreed to take the trip. He and his mother got along well. Brendon's father had died when he was young, and his mother had stepped into the role of a full-time parent. She'd taught him how to dance, how to cook, how to play piano, and how to clean in a way that made you believe things had never been dirty to begin with.

'Women don't want a man that will leave them with all of the housework. They also don't want men who will leave them bored,' she used to say. 'Take her out, sweep her off her feet, and when you take her home, continue to woo her. A man who can cook is a man worth keeping, a man who can play an instrument is a man who lights up your dreams, but a man who can do both? You'll be breaking hearts all over.'

It was, perhaps, an odd thing to drill into a child, but she had been right about some of it, at least. Just maybe not in the ways she'd hoped.

***

He arrived at his mother's house the following week. She gave him only an hour to settle in before dropping news of a dinner guest.

'Sabrina is a lovely young lady, I do think you'll quite like her. I've even made up the guest room down the hall for her in case she'd like to stay.'

So Brendon dressed in his best shirt, ready to meet his mother's guest. Upon her arrival, it became exceptionally clear that his mother had intended to set him up with this new friend. Despite his disinterest in any kind of relationship with the young woman, he introduced himself and found ways to hold up his side of the conversation. He did this with great caution, taking care not to encourage anything further.

After a satisfying meal of vegetables and rice, Brendon's mother excused herself and left the two alone.

'Your mother tells me you're a pianist. Would you play me something?' she asked softly, nodding at the piano on the far side of the room.

Brendon agreed. He made his way to the piano and began to play, so engrossed in the music that he hardly noticed a second body sliding onto the single-seat piano bench. Sabrina brushed her hand gently over his, startling him and snapping him out of his concentration. He relaxed his hands down into his lap and turned to face her.

'It's a beautiful instrument,' she whispered, her breath wafting far too close for comfort.

'Yes, it is,' he replied firmly, shifting over the few extra millimetres of space left behind him.

She reached a hand up, gently gripping the side of his jaw. He could see what was happening. Somehow, as much as he'd tried to remain neutral, she hadn't taken it, and now she was going to kiss him. But how could he make her stop? She'd backed him into a corner, and he'd found himself glued to the seat, unable to walk away without knocking her over in the rush.

He began to feel a slight tickle in his nose, a feeling that often came to him in times of great anxiety, and before he'd had time to do anything about it-

he sneezed.

Right in poor Sabrina's face.

Brendon felt awful, quickly reaching for the handkerchief he always kept folded in his pocket and offering it to her.

'My deepest apologies. I must be allergic to something. Your perfume, perhaps.'

Sabrina stood quickly, dabbing her face with the handkerchief until she was finally given directions to the bathroom. She returned a moment later with a freshly washed face, gently placing the handkerchief back in Brendon's hand before collecting her bag and saying her farewell.

***

The following day, Brendon's mother woke him with fresh scones and coffee for breakfast. She'd been in a rather foul mood after Sabrina's abrupt exit, but now it was as though the disastrous event had never occurred, and she was dashing about all smiles and cheer once more.

After they'd finished their meal, Brendon finally understood why his mother was so happy. The scones they'd had for breakfast weren't just any old supermarket scones; they'd come from a local bakery run by a young lady called Madeline, who just happened to be available for dinner that night.

While the man had no doubts Madeline was a wonderful woman, his mother's pressure on his love life was becoming more and more of a problem. He'd taken time away from his job, from the comfort of his home, and come to visit her, but all she seemed to care about was setting him up. It was possible she believed he was missing something by being alone, but he had never felt that way.

In fact, as far as he could recall, Brendon hadn't had a single crush in his life.

The girls he'd gone to school with had been pretty, sure. But he had never felt the desire to ask any of them out. He'd never met a girl he wanted to kiss. And marriage? This thing his mother seemed so incredibly fixated on? Marriage had not crossed his mind at all. Not naturally, that is.

And so he had never been able to understand his mother's incessant nagging over the matter, or why she insisted on pushing so hard for him to find a relationship.

It was likely his mother had given him notice so he could prepare for their guest and make himself as presentable and charming as he could. Instead, it had been the perfect opportunity to create a plan. Instead of charming his mother's suitors, he would find ways to repel them.

When Madeline arrived for dinner, Brendon's mother greeted her with an enthusiastic smile and a warm hug, as if they'd been friends for years.

Throughout the meal, Brendon's mother made countless attempts to drag him into the conversation, but he made minimal effort to engage. His responses were short and reserved, rarely inviting a follow-up, and not once did he initiate a topic. On top of his apparent lack of conversational skills, he barely looked at the young woman, opting to focus on his food or the scratches on the table.

By the end of the meal, Madeline had seen quite enough.

'I can see my presence here isn't wanted,' she spoke firmly. 'Thank you for the lovely meal, but your son has made his disinterest in me quite clear.' And with that, she was gone.

***

For the next few days, Brendon's mother continued to encourage him, trying to convince him to ask out the security guard at the supermarket, the young lady sitting alone in a cafe, and even the receptionist at her dentist's office, but was met with the same response each time.

It finally looked as though she had given up.

Then, on the final day of his visit, there was a knock on the door. Brendon's mother hadn't told him anyone would be coming over, so he stayed in his room, assuming it was a friend of hers who'd come to visit.

A few minutes later, his mother called him down.

'There's someone I'd like you to meet,' her voice rang down the hallway with the words he had come to dread.

Not in the mood for another of her attempts at setting him up, he trudged to the doorway, dropping a fake cough for good measure with every intention of feigning ill. But when Brendon looked up, he caught not the eyes of the young woman at the door, but those of the man beside her.

The man's eyes softened and he shared a smile that made Brendon's chest grow tight and his breath thick.

'Brendon,' his mother called, stealing his attention back. 'This is Emily and her brother, Pearson. Their car broke down, so rather than leave them to sit outside in the storm, I invited them to join us for dinner. Emily works in a bookstore. You love to read, don't you?'

But Brendon was only half-listening to his mother as she carried on about Emily. He was far more interested in their other guest.

'And you?' he asked softly, his gaze directed at Pearson.

'I'm a florist, actually.'

'Really? I've always wanted to know more about... florist... stuff.' Brendon cursed internally at his fumbled words. *How could he be so daft?*

The four of them shared a meal at the table. Emily had been strategically placed beside Brendon, likely with the hope that proximity would encourage a bond. But how could Brendon give all his attention to a woman he'd just met, when her brother, sitting across from him, kept looking at him with *those eyes*?

For the duration of the meal Brendon's mother, as was her habit, tried a little too hard to include him in her conversation with Emily, and while he was more cooperative than usual with his responses, he continued to swap glances with Pearson. Whenever his mother would drag him into the discussion, he would find a way to take Pearson with him.

After the first hour of swapping smiles and locking eyes, Brendon felt something brush against his ankle, accompanied by a subtle grin from Pearson. He suddenly felt himself overwhelmed with the feelings that had been skittering around his edges since they first caught each other's eyes. Feelings he couldn't recall ever having felt before. All of this softness, the fluttering in his chest, and the *longing*.

His mother's interruptions gradually died down as he and the man across from him found their way deeper into their own conversation. She had never seen her son so interactive before. It wasn't like him to be particularly social or invested in those around him, but she could tell he was awfully fond of the young man. She had never seen him smile like this, and never as much as he had that night.

Upon her realisation, Brendon's mother invited Emily to a different room, giving the two men some space to make their own choices without feeling influenced.

Brendon and Pearson spent the whole night talking and getting to know each other and in the morning they went out for breakfast. Just the two of them.

'I don't mind who you're with, as long as you're happy and well,' his mother said when he told her. She'd only ever wanted the best for her son, even if she'd been a little off the mark in her efforts.

***

When it was time for Brendon to head home, Pearson went with him. At first, he had only a few days off from his flower shop but he soon began to look for work closer to his love. After a couple of weeks, he'd decided to relocate and set up a new shop, right across the street from Brendon's store.

They would have lunch together every day, and show each other the stars at night.

A few months later, Brendon rushed to his florist.

'My mother always hoped for a princess, but now I've found my prince. You are all I've ever needed. Will you marry me?'

'Of course,' Pearson answered, smiling brighter than ever. 'Marrying you is more than I could have dreamed for.'

Brendon and Pearson were wed several weeks later in a local garden with their closest friends and family.

They adopted a rescue dog, a beautiful border collie named Princess.

And when Brendon's twenty-fifth birthday came around, he was spoiled with gifts.

But the best one of all

was Pearson.

Lights

December 22nd

Ash paced between the front window and the desk on the far side of the room, anxiously flinging his arms around. His best friend sat on the couch, nibbling on a candy cane as he watched his friend spiral.

'Just sit down. I came over because you said we would watch a movie. I expected to watch a *movie*, not you,' Fern whined, slipping not-so-gracefully onto the floor. 'Please come help me pick a movie, at least. Are we gonna watch a Christmas one, or something else?'

'I will. In a sec. I just wanted to check the lights were on.'

'Ash. The lights are fine. You've checked them seven times in the past five minutes. It's still early. Besides, it's only the twenty-second. Most people go out on the twenty-fourth. *Please.*'

Ash stopped pacing and looked over at his friend. He was right, they had planned to watch a movie together. But this was the first time he'd been able to put up decorations. He'd never been allowed when he was living with his family, but now he had his own place and everything seemed stable, and he realised *no one could stop him*. So he did it. They weren't brilliant, but they were *his* and he was excited. The lights had always been the best part of

Christmas, and with his family in the state that it was now, the lights were all he had left.

But Fern was right. He'd come over so they could watch a Christmas movie together, and they had quite a list to choose from.

'What are you in the mood for? Is there a specific one you wanna watch, or...?'

'I'm not sure. It seems like you could use a solid distraction though, so I'm thinking either comedy or action might be our best options. Comedy keeps you hooked, but action means you kinda *have* to pay attention to know what's going on. Best distraction material,' Fern said as he flicked through the pile of DVDs on the floor.

'Sounds good,' Ash mumbled, still thinking about the lights.

Focus, Ash. Just breathe.

'Television, Fern's bag, hallway, remotes, jigsaw,' Ash whispered softly. 'Couch, carpet, clothes, and... cushions. Traffic, screaming, and Fern flicking through the DVDs. Tinsel and potato. Chocolate, lingering from twenty minutes earlier.' He closed his eyes and took a deep breath.

'I've got it!' Fern yelled a few minutes later. 'Actually, I had it before, but you were doing the counting thing so I just kept looking and... anyway! Lethal Weapon. Perfect combination of action and comedy that is so very much needed at this moment, but also a very solid Christmas movie.'

Ash nodded in agreement, Fern crawled over to put the disc in, and the two boys watched the movie with a record-low of only three interruptions and pauses. Any potential crisis was postponed to another day.

December 23rd

'I think this is going to be the last year I do Christmas,' Ash said as he gazed out the window at the hint of an incoming storm. 'I mean, I've been wanting to get out of it for years, but it's been hard to get people to *let me* stay out of it.'

'Just not feeling holly-jolly and merry anymore?' Fern asked, spinning absently on the desk chair.

'Well, it's a little bit that, I guess. But there are a lot of reasons. It just doesn't feel like it makes sense to keep doing it when I have so many reasons *not* to.'

Fern nodded, tipping a little as the chair began to slow.

'Like, it's mostly for the kids, right? And I am not a kid, nor do I have any. And since I'm not going to the family get-together anymore, what am I doing it for at all? It's not for them, and it's certainly not for me, so it just seems like a waste.'

'That makes sense.'

'Sure, it could be argued that it's an excuse to see the family you don't get a chance to see otherwise, but again, I'm not included in the get-together, so this feels redundant.'

'Solid point.'

'And yesterday, someone came into the shop and she was talking to Marla about the Carols event and started complaining that the group performing wasn't allowed to sing Christmas carols because it's apparently illegal because of the religious aspect. Then she started going on about how that's bullshit because Christmas is a religious holiday and if they're not religious they should just stay out of it, which I have several issues with, but the focus point is that I'm the most anti-religious person I know, so it really doesn't make sense that I keep being forced into the event.'

'Yeah.' Fern stopped spinning.

'And it's also bullshit because if they have such an issue with people who aren't part of their religion being involved in the event, and if they really truly believe people who aren't part of the religion should "just stay out of it", then why do they make it so impossible to avoid? It's plastered *everywhere*. It's inescapable. They fill every shop with it, put it all over town with decorations, they play music in the plazas, it's on TV and in every advertisement and you literally cannot go anywhere without seeing it, hearing about it, or someone mentioning it in a conversation. And yet, we all know that if any other group or religion tried to make something even a tenth as public and widely promoted as Christmas is, everyone would *lose their ever-loving shit*. That would be shut down *so fast*, but it isn't, because no one would ever dare speak against the *oh so high and mighty Christians*.'

Ash had stood up again somewhere in the midst of his ranting and was back to pacing the room. Energy was desperate to escape from every inch of his bones as he flung his arms all around.

'And *another thing*,' he yelled. 'Kids are constantly being told not to accept things from strangers. It's drilled into them at every possible moment, *and yet* here we are telling them Santa is fine, and anyone that *looks* like Santa is fine, and that it's totally safe and cool to eat whatever any Santa-esque being gives you at an event, and that it's absolutely normal for this complete stranger to not only spy on you every second of every moment of your life, but that he will break into your house while you're asleep. Like, don't take anything from strangers and definitely don't eat it, but *oh this is fine because it's freaking Santa*.'

'Right!' Fern cried out. 'No, that's exactly it. Because... what the fuck is that? And it's not just a mystery guy, because they've created this image of him and now kids just walk up to anyone that looks and dresses that way and assume he's safe. It's so contradictory.'

'Exactly. The whole thing is a giant pile of contradictions. And it's so normalised. "If you're not religious, just stay out of it" Okay, so why is the event so heavily directed at children?'

'Socially acceptable mass indoctrination,' Fern sang.

Ash shoots finger guns in response. 'Nailed it.'

The pair sat in silence for a moment, allowing some time for the energy of the last few minutes to recuperate. It was a lot, but things with the most weight are often the things that most need to be said.

'So, yeah. There are a lot of reasons, really, and it's something I've been thinking about for several years. Even before all this shit happened and got me cut out of all celebrations. It's just... we have such limited time here, why should I put so much energy into something that only causes stress and exhaustion? *Merry* Christmas, my ass. More like *misery*.'

They smiled softly at each other across the room. Sadness drifted delicately between them, but it was comfortable. Accepted.

'Does that mean *all* of Christmas?' Fern asked quietly.

'What do you mean?'

'Well, there's the family stuff, sure, and the gifts, but there are also work events and... decorations.'

Ash felt a heavy pull inside his chest and flicked his eyes back to the window. His window. The display he'd spent several hours on after realising he had the freedom to put things up. He thought about the nights spent as a child wandering with family members and friends, looking at all the lights and displays. The way he would yell "Shinies!" whenever they drove past even the smallest setups. Such a simple thing that brought so much joy, and he'd only ever wanted to return the favour and be the one to cast smiles upon faces that would otherwise lie dormant and forlorn.

But Fern was right. The lights were part of Christmas, and if he was giving up Christmas, surely that meant the lights would have to go too.

December 24th

'Fern, you're not going to believe this,' Ash blurted as soon as he heard the cessation of the dial tone. He was peeking through the curtain, watching in shock as two more cars pulled up and people unfolded out of them to join the small crowd outside his house. 'There are people here. So many people. Looking at my lights.'

'I'll be there soon. How are you for candy canes? Y'know what, I'll just grab some,' Fern replied with a smile in his voice.

Ash went to change his shirt. Instead of snowmen, this shirt had sandmen. Since it only snowed in a few places, and that only happened in the middle of winter (certainly not at Christmas when the sun was blazing down the way it did), sandmen made a lot more sense. Instead of scarves and beanies, they wore sunglasses and broad-brimmed hats, and their features were made with rocks and shells. He slipped it on, grabbed the packet of candy canes he'd abandoned on the kitchen bench, and headed outside.

The crowd had grown now, with some people waiting further back until they could move forward for a closer look. Ash couldn't believe it. He'd only put up a few strands of lights in his loungeroom window, and a few decorations on the inside. Most people only stopped for large house-wide, yard-filling displays, never the smaller ones. But here they all were, crowding closer, taking photos, laughing and chatting away.

Fern came jogging down the footpath towards him, flailing a bag full of packets of candy canes.

'I got... more... candy canes,' he said between gasps. 'Mum had to... park... around the corner... because of the cars.' He dropped down onto the concrete driveway and fell flat on his back, lazily pointing to his mouth before letting his arm fall across his chest.

Ash darted inside to grab a drink for his friend, and a bucket for the candy canes. When Fern had recovered from running the width of two houses, they put the candy canes into the bucket, hanging some in a pattern around the edge with the rest dumped inside, and began to offer them around. A few people came up to tell Ash how much they liked his display and told him he'd done a great job. His chest ached with cosy feelings and his skin tingled with wonder; he'd never imagined so many people would come.

They spent a while handing out candy canes and talking to visitors who'd appeared to look at Ash's lights. They spoke to kids about their Christmas wishes, they spoke to adults about their plans for the day, and they accepted many compliments on what Ash had believed was a display too simple for anyone to care about. But cars pulled up from all over town, and out poured people of all ages. One group had even come from a neighbouring town.

When the crowds had dimmed and most people were getting back into their cars, the two boys made their way inside the house and sat together on the loungeroom floor.

'I don't understand,' Ash mumbled. 'I mean, I'm glad it's making people happy, but it's such a small display. These people could have gone *anywhere*, but they came to me, to my silly little lights.'

He heard a noise beside him, building up slowly until Fern erupted into a fit of giggles and pulled his phone out of his pocket. He tapped away for a moment before turning the screen to show Ash what he'd done. It was a post Fern had made in the local Christmas lights group.

Hey folks

My friend has put up some lights this year. They're not much, it's not a huge fancy display, but it's his first time putting up lights (or anything festive) and he's really worried no one will come.

I know it's only a small display, but he put a lot into it and he's really excited about it, so if you're in the area I know it would mean the world to him if one or two people came by and stopped to look at lights.

see attached photo

'Fern, I-'

'I know how much the lights meant to you, and I wanted to make sure you were able to share that with the people it was for. I thought maybe a few people might drop by on their way past, but this... sometimes people can be amazing. They can prove us wrong and do things we never would have expected. Merry Final Christmas, Ash.' Fern grinned, and if Ash's heart wasn't already full, this alone would have filled it.

'Thank you.'

'Also,' Fern said, drawing it out, 'I did a little bit of research. I mean, I thought I knew, but I wanted to be sure before I told you and got your hopes up or anything. But anyway, there's no reason you should have to stop putting up lights. Christians try to push that it's to symbolise the birth of Jesus, *he is the son who brings us light* or whatever, but, as usual, they stole the symbolism and twisted it to suit their narrative. Heh, narrative... because it's based on a book.' He took a break to laugh at his unintentional pun before continuing. '*Anyway*, the point is, that's not what it's about.'

'Fern. Breathe. What *is* it about?'

'The sun.' He beamed. 'The lights symbolise the birth of the sun. That big ball of light in the sky. Well, technically they weren't around then, but lights at this time of year are used to symbolise... light. I guess they used candles then. But now we have these, and they're pretty and they're less of a hazard and they don't smell awful, so they're infinitely better than candles.'

'Light symbolises light. Who would've guessed.'

'Yeah. Well. I mean, it's not *exact*, and that's probably a simplified version. But I thought maybe it would help to know that. Y'know? So, maybe this doesn't have to be the last year you put up lights, maybe next year they can just mean something different.'

'Maybe they can,' Ash whispered. 'Thank you.'

He leaned back against the front of the couch and closed his eyes. Everything had gotten so busy with the amount of people that had shown up. The talking, the smiling, the cosiness bubbling inside him... it was *a lot*.

But it was worth it. All the excited children running around. All the people saying "*Wow!*" as they looked at what he'd done. All of the smiles and laughter, all broad and grinning and bright.

And he made it happen.

He'd done it. He'd given them joy.

Santa's Beard

November 25th

Mrs Claus glanced at her husband, passed out in an armchair by the fire, residue of fallen tears still clinging to his cheeks. She had spent many years loving him, and her love was not something that had been known to fade, but the kind of love he needed was something she could never give him. They'd been together since they were young because that's what it was like then. But times were changing; maybe it didn't have to be that way now.

When Santa first came to be, way back in the beginning, the original Santa was straight. Everyone before him was too, all his predecessors, generation after generation.

Until now.

Following tradition, Santa and Mrs Claus had come from the same village. Santa, being born into his role, was to marry the first girl he fell in love with. This girl would become Mrs Claus.

But this time, they weren't in love. They were close, for sure, but they could only ever be close as friends. She cared for him and loved him as much as she could love anyone, and he loved her the same as a sister. They got on well, they did their jobs, they made children and others around the world smile and feel joy, and everything was worth it.

But it was getting to him, no matter how hard he tried to push through and hide it.

Today they'd been at a photo shoot, one of the first main advertising campaigns for the year. Everything was going well, the set had been lovely, and it was comfortable (something they'd found wasn't too common with these events). The photographer had arranged a beautiful display beside a barn, snow covering the ground, tinsel hanging from the roof (properly attached so it wouldn't fall where the animals might eat it), a Christmas tree to one side of the scene (out of reach of the reindeer on the other side), and a comfortable two-seater couch right in the middle. They'd taken a couple of shots decorating the tree, a few more with the reindeer, patting and feeding him, and were then instructed to sit together on the couch. A couple of cute shots drinking tea, one where Mrs Claus had held out a biscuit for Santa to take a bite out of, and another where they sat close with an arm around each other.

Everything had been fine.

That is, until the photographer requested a shot of them sharing a kiss.

At first, they'd had a quick laugh at the idea and kissed each other on the cheek, but the photographer had told them that wasn't what he'd meant. Mrs Claus believed it would have been alright if they'd simply said they weren't comfortable with the idea and moved on. *If only that was how it had played out*, she thought. Instead, Santa had panicked. He didn't want to kiss Mrs Claus, she was his best friend, but how could he explain that without disclosing the lack of validity in their relationship? He was a fraud! A liar! He hid the truth not only from those close to him but the entire world! *How could he?*

Instead, he had simply excused himself to the bathroom, leaving Mrs Claus to wait. The photographer continued to explain that he needed something real, something *passionate*.

'Sure, they want to see Santa Claus. But they also want to see him happy. They want to know he's real, and to see him together with his true love,' the photographer exclaimed. He'd said it to Mrs Claus, as what he'd thought was encouragement. What he hadn't realised, was that Santa was on his way back and that overhearing the statement upon his return was the ultimate breaking point.

'I'm afraid we'll have to cut this short,' he said, heading back to his wife, gently taking her arm. 'I must have eaten something that's not quite agreeing with me.'

They'd spoken about it once they were home. It first came up a couple of years earlier, right around his thirtieth birthday Santa was going through a patch and he'd been incredibly down. He hadn't been sleeping, he'd barely been eating, and it got to a point where the workshop had been empty for weeks. Finally, Mrs Claus had approached him. She made sure he knew he could talk to her about anything. It took a few days, but he soon opened up and explained his feelings to her, but he had insisted they kept it a secret because he didn't want to be the one who let down the world and broke a tradition that had gone on for generations.

But lately, it seemed as though it was weighing on him more and more each day.

Mrs Claus turned away from her husband, back to her knitting, and sighed. She only wished there was something she could do to help him...

***

When December began, so would the festivities. Carols playing in the shops, decorations on houses and storefronts, events in parks and libraries, parties for workplaces, and, of course, shopping centre Santas. Everywhere you went was filled with colour, the sound of bells, and people in a mad rush to find the perfect gifts in the small gaps they had away from work. It was absolute chaos, but to Mrs Claus, it was home. It was comfort. It was everything she'd spent her life working for.

During this period, while Santa was overseeing toy construction and maintenance, Mrs Claus went out to join the celebrations, dropping by shopping centres to check in on the actors playing the in-store Santas, and giving a little extra encouragement to those who needed it. Of course, they didn't know she was married to the real Santa, but it often gave them more confidence to know they weren't out there alone.

Due to her husband's recent state, she'd decided not to go out as frequently as she had in previous years. Sunday of every week would be enough. She could spend the rest of the week doing errands, attending the occasional meeting, and helping out wherever she could.

Santa's depression had been taking more of a toll, and he'd been skipping meetings and taking days off from work with an increasing frequency. Mrs Claus had tried everything she knew that could help him. All of the things that had helped since they were children, any advice she could get from friends, exercises from her therapist, and even a few things she'd seen online. None of it helped.

But she had one last idea left.

This year, while she was out checking in on the store Santas, she was going to find her husband a boyfriend.

December 3rd

On the first weekend, she went out to the busiest plaza in a large city. This particular location was often one of her first stops, as it received a lot of traffic, often to the point where kids were getting turned away at closing time after standing in line for hours. Mrs Claus liked to walk along the lines, introducing herself to children and their families, taking some of the load off the acting Santa, and giving more people the opportunity they likely would have otherwise missed out on. While many of them would have preferred to meet Santa, she was a mighty fine alternative.

As expected, the place was packed before the store Santa had even shown up for his shift. Most stores were only just beginning to set up for the day, but the line for photographs was already taking up half of the food court.

Two minutes before the setup was due to open, a middle-aged man with blond hair ducked in the back door, carrying a gym bag. Exactly on the hour, Santa emerged from the small cottage, waving to the crowd on his way to the large red throne.

'Ho, ho ho!' he cheered in a booming voice.

The crowd screamed and hooted in response, and he settled down as security elves ushered the first child through the gate.

Mrs Claus watched from the side of the artificial yard, taking notes and talking with parents while the children got their photos taken. By lunchtime, they'd seen almost three hundred children, and everyone could agree the break was well-earned.

Before heading off for the day, Mrs Claus always stopped for a chat, often during Santa's lunch break. It never lasted as long as they hoped, especially when they had costumes to worry about, but it gave her a chance to get to know the actors a little better.

The cottages were set up with a table and some chairs, and a small changing room off to one side. This Santa was a regular actor, so he was able to get in and out of his costume in under a minute. When he walked out of the room and joined her with his lunch, no one would ever have guessed he was the same man who'd been greeting the children a moment earlier.

'So, you do a lot of acting? Only seasonal roles, or are you a performer as well?' Mrs Claus asked as she dipped a biscuit in her tea.

'Ah, I pick up gigs here and there,' the man replied. 'I can't stray too far, so I'm a bit limited for roles. Gotta stay local for the kids and missus. I do trade work when I'm not acting.'

'Oh, yes. Children are definitely worth sticking around for.' She gave him a soft smile. 'How old are they?'

'Four and seven. We've got another one on the way, so I've been picking up some extra jobs wherever I can. Though I cut it a bit close this morning, rocking up when I did. I was helping someone move a few things and it took a little longer than expected.'

'You still made it though, and no one seemed to mind.'

'For sure. But I think from now on I'll try and give myself a bit more time, just to be safe.'

'That sounds like an excellent idea. Better to be safe, as they say.' She held out the tin of biscuits for him to select one before placing it carefully in her bag. 'I'll be heading off soon, I'm only around for a few hours. Lots to do, you know.'

'I bet,' he said with a chuckle. 'I'm Samuel, by the way. Thanks for all the help today. It was lovely to meet you, uh...'

'You can call me Mrs Claus,' she replied sweetly as she stood, picking up her bag and heading out the door.

December 10th

A week later, Mrs Claus headed to a smaller town a few hours away from the city. There she met Charlie, who appeared to be going for the record of *most unkempt Santa*. He showed up almost twenty minutes late, drenched in sweat and reeking of a recent cigarette. The red suit he wore hung loosely over his body, covered in stains and coming unstitched under the sleeves.

Throughout the day, Mrs Claus watched as children approached the scene filled with hope and excitement only to walk away disappointed and let down. Almost a third of the children who visited walked away in tears. Charlie (you could hardly call him Santa) repeatedly pulled down his beard to scratch his chin or wipe his nose on his sleeve, and he had to be reminded constantly to ensure both of his hands were visible during photos.

Mrs Claus decided to stick around longer this time. Not for the sake of Charlie, but for the children and their families. Some of the children even opted to see her instead of the not-so-jolly man in the red suit.

By the middle of the afternoon, he'd become so agitated that the rest of the group decided to shut down early and call it a day. Most kids had been seen by that point anyway, and the parents of those who remained appeared relieved by the announcement. Once the civilians in the area had cleared out, the owners of the store approached Charlie about his presentation.

The last thing Mrs Claus saw on her way out was Charlie throwing his beard down as he shouted profanities at the approaching security guards.

December 17th

On the third weekend, Mrs Claus met a store Santa with thick, blocky eyebrows, a cropped jacket, and a carefully sculpted beard. He spoke in a soft voice and wore heeled shoes to compensate for his lack of natural height.

'Ohh, no,' he'd said when she first arrived, pulling her to the side. 'Listen, I don't know who sent you, but we have our own Mrs Claus coming in today. You're welcome to stick around for the show, but we can't have you performing. I'm so sorry to have wasted your time.'

'Oh, not at all,' she replied. 'I'm just drifting. I pass through and visit store Santas, give help where it's needed, and observe where it isn't. I'm certainly not here to be in the way.'

'Excellent! It's lovely to meet you, I've gotta run, but George here will set you up in a spot close to the stage.' He snapped his fingers at a man with close-cut black hair and a thin beard. 'George, could we please have a VIP seat for this lovely lady?' George nodded and the Santa stalked off to the other side of the room.

'A stage? That's different,' Mrs Claus said to George as he showed her to her seat.

'It certainly is, ma'am. The show really is something special, I hope you enjoy it.' His voice was deep and rough, and every word made her feel a little more at ease. 'If you need anything else, give me a wave.'

He walked back the way he'd come, glancing back on his way through the door. She could've sworn she'd seen him wink.

The lights dimmed a second later and she felt better knowing no one would be able to see her blush. That wasn't what she was there for. Besides, a man as fine as George was bound to be already taken.

Then the music started, loud and filled with beats and vibrations. Multicoloured spotlights spun around the room, smaller lights flashing on the stage as fog machines blew out a cloud across the doorway. A figure emerged through the fog, one hand on his hip, the other waving a bedazzled cane.

The Santa trotted around the stage, calling out to the crowd to hype them up as he made his way from one side to the other. He gave Mrs Claus a sneaky wave when he reached her side, then headed back to the middle.

'I think we have a special visitor here tonight. Does anybody know her name?' he cried out.

The crowd screamed in response.

'I can't hear you, maybe we need to get a little more *energy* in here. Don't you want to meet my wife?'

The crowd screamed again, louder this time.

'Ooh, I'm not sure that's good enough,' he teased. 'You know the missus, enthusiasm and attention are her *life force*. Now, one last time, let me hear you *scream!*'

The crowd went wild, screaming and hollering all around, and a few whistles went off around the room.

And then she emerged. Strutting onto the stage with her bold makeup, sparkly red dress, and the highest heels Mrs Claus had ever seen in her life.

'Mrs Claws is here, baby!' she hollered, stretching out an exaggeratedly manicured hand. 'That's c-l-a-w-s, for all you newbies. Mrow!'

***

After the show, George came back to collect Mrs Claus and take her backstage to officially meet the performers. He offered her his arm to escort her, and she accepted, biting her lip to hide a smile.

Mrs Claws looked up as they approached. 'Ooh, darling, is this the one you were telling me about? What a cutie!'

The Santa hurried over, holding out a hand. 'Sorry I had to rush off earlier without a proper introduction. My name is Earnest, as in Hemingslay, and this is Miss Nikita Cupcakes. How did you cope with the show? Was it too much?'

'I've never seen anything like it,' Mrs Claus said with a wide grin.

'Oh, but did it *slay* or should it *be slayed*?' Nikita asked.

Before she had time to frown, George stepped in. 'What they mean, is did you enjoy it?'

'I thought it was brilliant. A very special performance, indeed.' She glanced at George intending to thank him, and caught him staring at her, a soft smile resting on his face. Her blush returned, and this time there was nothing to hide it.

'We're so glad you liked it! Thanks for sticking around, we know it's not everyone's cup of tea,' Earnest said. 'How would you feel about grabbing lunch?'

'Ah, actually,' Nikita chimed, not giving anyone else a chance to process what was said, let alone respond. 'We've got another performance across town, so we've gotta run. Right, babe?'

'I mean, that's not for a while yet, I think we've got ti-'

Nikita nudged him with her elbow and flicked her head towards Mrs Claus, her eyes darting like flashing arrows to the arm that was still wrapped up in George's.

'Ohh.' Earnest smiled. 'Yeah. Sorry, gotta run. It was lovely to meet you. Maybe another time.'

Nikita grabbed his arm and began to drag him away, winking at Mrs Claus on her way past.

Unsure what to say or do next, Mrs Claus stayed silent. When she realised she was still holding George's arm, she panicked, jumping back and almost tripping over her own feet. George reached out to keep her steady.

'Are you alright?'

'Yes, thank you. I'm sorry, I didn't mean to cling to you the way I did, that wasn't particularly well-mannered of me.'

'It's alright,' he spoke softly, then smiled at her. 'The company was quite welcome. Actually, if you've got some time, perhaps we could grab a coffee?'

Mrs Claus felt a ping, almost a flutter, deep inside her chest. She checked the time, hoping it would allow her to stay just a little longer, but she'd already been out later than she'd planned. 'I really should be getting home soon. I've got a few things I need to take care of. Someone to check in on.'

'My apologies, I did not mean to overstep. Whoever it is, they're very lucky to have you.' He took a small step back, giving her a little extra space.

'I would though. Like to. One day, just not today. Perhaps I could give you my number?' A mix of hope and unease stirred around her, watching as he pulled a notebook out of his pocket and wrote his own down, before passing her the book to do the same.

'You're safe, right?' he asked carefully, his voice laced with concern.

'Safe? Yes, of course. I just need to focus on helping out a friend before I make time for anything else. It's complicated, but not remotely unsafe,' she explained. The world couldn't know who she was, and she'd made a promise to keep her husband's secret, so she had to be careful with what she said and how things were phrased. Complicated pretty much covered it, she thought.

'I can handle complicated,' George said with a friendly wink. 'Whatever you need, however you need it, I can find a way. Take care, Mrs Claus. Until we meet again.'

He leaned over and kissed her gently on the cheek, and she watched as he walked away.

December 24th

Mrs Claus almost didn't leave the house on the final Sunday before Christmas. There was so much to do, and she'd had no luck in her mission so far. Santa was rushing around making all sorts of last-minute plans and putting together ideas with barely enough time for the execution. He was tripping over himself, and all she could do was try her very darndest not to get in the way. They'd only been up an hour before she decided she was far better off being anywhere else in the world.

So she opted for one final outing, one last attempt to make something good before the season came to an end, and she found herself in a small city plaza with a roped-off corner in the food court for Santa's chair. There was no cottage, no change room, no security elves. Just the store Santa, a photographer, and a large chair.

A young woman sat at the nearest table, engrossed in a book. When the crowd died down, she went to the edge of the roped area.

'Hey, babe, I'm gonna go grab something to eat. Did you need anything? Coffee? A snack?'

'I'm all good, I brought some water with me,' the store Santa replied. He watched her as she started towards the cafe, then turned to Mrs Claus. 'No one said anything about extra actors. I guess they didn't tell you how quiet it gets here either. Some days we're lucky if five kids show up.'

Part of her wanted to leave. It was quiet, there were no kids to help, and she'd failed at her mission. The one thing she'd set out hoping to achieve, and she'd failed. It nagged at her, knowing she might be letting down someone so important to her. But something else was latching on, telling her to stay.

'That's alright. I'm more of a passerby at any rate. Not in any specific place for any specific reason, simply dropping in and helping out where I'm needed,' she told him with a smile.

'Well, you're welcome to stick around. Pull up a chair, or you can sit with Sarah when she comes back. I'll warn you though, she can be quite chatty. I'm Noah, by the way.'

'It's lovely to meet you, Noah.' She looked up at the group heading towards them. 'It looks like you've got a few visitors on the way.'

Since he didn't get a lot of traffic, Mrs Claus decided it was best if she kept out of the way and let Noah do his job. She took up the suggestion to sit with Sarah, who'd brought back an extra berry scone.

'Are you sure Noah won't want it?'

'He's not a scone guy. You looked like a scone lady. I did have to guess on the flavour, so I hope it's alright.'

Mrs Claus wasn't sure what it meant to look like a scone person, but she had to admit it had been a rather accurate assumption. 'That's very sweet, thank you. He's very lucky to have a girlfriend as lovely as you.'

Sarah sputtered, catching small pieces of pastry in her hand as she tried to stop her laughter. 'I'm not his girlfriend.'

'Oh, I apologise,' Mrs Claus said quickly, feeling a heat grow in her cheeks as she realised her mistake. 'You just seemed so close, and the way you referred to him earlier made me think you must be together. I shouldn't have made that assumption.'

'That's totally okay. It happens a lot. We've been friends since we were nine, so we are really close. He's gay though, so that kinda throws a spanner in the works.'

Wait.

'And his boyfriend doesn't mind you using those terms with him?' Mrs Claus asked.

Sarah smirked. 'He doesn't have a boyfriend. And even if he did, it's not up to someone else to tell him how to live or who to be friends with.'

'You know what, Sarah? I think you're absolutely right. People should be free to be who they are and love who they love.' Mrs Claus broke off a piece of her scone and chewed it thoughtfully. 'How would you like to help me out with something? There's someone I'd like to introduce Noah to. If you think he'd be up for it.'

December 27th

Because Christmas was a busy day for everyone, and Boxing Day was often set aside as a day to recover from the month-long buildup for the busiest day of the year, Mrs Claus had decided to invite everyone for dinner the day after. Sarah had been on board with the plan right away and had convinced Noah to have dinner with Mrs Claus and her husband. After spending the afternoon chatting, gossiping, and scheming, they finally had a plan. She'd also convinced Mrs Claus to consider inviting George, and, after checking with her husband, she did just that.

'Of course,' Santa had said when she'd asked him. 'You've done all of this for me, you should be able to invite whoever you like. See where it goes.'

'I didn't want to do too much at once, or make anything awkward.'

'Nothing could ever be awkward. Not with us.' He smiled at her, his face lined with adoration. 'And if you need someone to give him, or any future suitors, a talking to, make sure he treats you right, I'd be more than happy to take up that role.'

The five of them got together and had a brilliant dinner, pieced together with a little bit of everyone's leftovers from the big event.

Sarah had taken over and spent the evening dashing around, refilling everyone's drinks and keeping conversations going. Not that they'd had much trouble

George had brought fresh flowers from his neighbour's garden, and Mrs Claus found herself fighting harder than ever not to melt right down into a puddle. They'd arranged another date, just the two of them, for early January.

Santa and Noah had been the best part of all. They'd hit it off instantly, barely stopping for a breath between sentences all night. At times, it almost seemed as if they'd forgotten anyone else was there. After dinner, they'd gone for a walk around the yard together, and Sarah almost had to drag Noah to the car when it came time to leave. Mrs Claus hadn't seen Santa smile like that in years.

After everyone had left, he turned and pulled her into a hug, tears streaming down his cheeks.

'Thank you. This was the best gift anyone could have given me,' he whispered. '*You* are the best gift *life* could have given me. I got to have my first kiss tonight. A real one. You have no idea how much that means.'

But she knew. She could see it on his face, hear it in the cracks in his voice, and feel it in the subtle shifts in his body as she held him. She'd always known, and that was why she'd done it.

Because everybody deserves the chance to love someone and be loved.

And because it's never too late to do what makes you happy.

Finding Colours

Emery sat on her bed, legs crossed, staring solemnly at the pile of blank and abandoned canvases on the floor. Rows of tubs lined the shelves along the wall, all filled to the brim with various paints and art supplies. The one consistent love in her life, left untouched, collecting dust for months and months.

At first, it was excusable. She'd been away, staying in a town a few hours from home where she was studying art at TAFE because her local campus didn't run creative courses. There had been a unit with affordable rent a few blocks away, making it easy for her to get to her classes on time without any extra cost.

But what was her excuse now? She'd been home for weeks, and everything was still in the same place it had been when she first left. It was all too much to think about. Every time she tried, it felt as though a thousand weights were slowly drifting down on top of her, crushing everything inside. She thought studying art was the right thing to do, but instead of giving her a space to improve and fall further in love, it had ripped out the love that had been there like a weed and poisoned the soil underneath.

Art could never be something she hated, but it had become more of a demand. Studying a subject wasn't always the same as loving it, and most of the work was tedious. Day in, day out, each one filled with repetition and lectures about how some long-dead man would paint a certain way to achieve greatness and everyone new must follow in his footsteps if they ever wanted to be worth something. With each passing day, the course was taking more from her soul-well to fill its own cup.

It was striving for perfection, but all of her strokes had waves.

It was begging for perfection, but her canvas had bumps and ridges.

It was screaming for perfection, but she could no longer listen.

Her fingers ran gently up and down the seam on her pillow as she continued to stare down at the floor. They longed to pick up a brush, a crayon, a pencil, *anything*... but lately all she'd been able to do was wait.

She took a deep breath, throwing the pillow back to the top of the bed.

She was done waiting.

Emery slid from the bed onto the floor and dragged a small black case out of her backpack. Next, she pulled a sketchbook from the top of the pile under her desk, flipping through the pages in search of the next blank one. She put the tip of her pencil to the page and stared at the white space in front of her. No one could say how long she sat like this, but eventually, after a few almost-starts, she figured out how to begin.

***

Paper clung to her face, the ridges from the coil impressed in her cheek. Hours had passed. It was dark outside, and she could hear her mum and brother in the kitchen, the smell of Chinese takeaway drifting through the house. She pulled herself up slowly, careful not to damage the pages she'd been working on all afternoon.

'What happened to your face?' a voice called from the doorway.

'I fell asleep on my sketchbook. What's your excuse?' she fired back with a smirk.

Danny chuckled, his teeth showing in the middle of his lopsided grin. He was only three years younger than her, but sometimes that gap between them felt blurred, as if the universe had changed its mind about keeping them separated, but it was too late to erase from the sketch. 'Mum got dinner. She said she hopes you're hungry because it was very busy today and we almost left but she didn't want to cook and neither did I and we both know better than to ask you.'

'Oi! I can cook.'

'Yeah, but neither of us were in the mood for spreads on toast for dinner.' He laughed again, running back to the kitchen before she could respond.

When she arrived in the kitchen, her mum passed her a plate, already loaded up with her favourite things. Danny was sitting in his usual spot, picking at the rice in his sectioned plate. Their mum had found it in a kitchenware store a few years ago, and he'd hardly used anything different since. He hated it when his wet food came into contact with his side food. Emery liked hers side-by-side, but it didn't matter too much if they overlapped a little in the middle. Neither of them had ever understood why it was the standard to put one food on top of the other.

It was a quiet night at the table, as it often was after one of Danny's appointments. The psychologist their doctor had all but demanded they take him to wasn't the worst he'd seen, but it still took a lot out of him. Emery sometimes wondered if it might have been making things worse.

'Emery, what's all over your face?' their mum asked, a loaded fork paused in front of her mouth.

'I, uh-'

'She fell asleep on her sketchbook,' Danny blurted.

'Oh, you've been doing some drawing again? I was getting a bit worried for a while there, all that stuff of yours sitting untouched like that. I guess the course is taking up all that creative energy, is it?'

Fuck. That vice gripping her heart tightened again. Her throat suddenly felt too thick to swallow as she thought about all those things she hadn't said.

'Mum,' Emery whispered, setting down her fork. 'I need to tell you something.' Her mum and brother were both looking at her now, expecting something, waiting for her to speak. She'd dropped out months ago, all this time spent avoiding the subject, dodging questions, praying they'd simply forget as time went by. 'I dropped out of my course. It happened a while ago. I'm sorry I didn't tell you sooner, I just didn't know how.'

'Oh, sweetheart, it's okay. Do you need to move back in with us? What about your lease?'

'My lease ran out a bit over a month ago.'

'A month? You've only been here a couple of weeks. Emery, where have you been sleeping all this time?'

'With a friend. That's why I've been coming back more often. I knew I needed to tell you, and I know I should have sooner but I just couldn't.'

'It's alright. You're here. You're safe. That's what matters.'

'I know dropping out probably wasn't the right thing to do, I'm so sorry.'

'Hey. Sometimes the right thing for everyone else isn't always the right thing for us. If this is what you needed to do, that's okay.' Her mum reached a hand across the table and gently touched her arm. 'Was it just getting to be a bit too much?'

'Mum,' Emery sobbed. 'It was killing me.'

***

The next morning, Emery pulled herself out of bed with a tiny spark of hope buried under the ashes in her heart. A spark that had been hiding for so long, but something big enough to be the starting point for a flame nonetheless. She was going to paint something today. She didn't know what just yet, but she was going to try.

After dinner, Danny had left them alone at the table and headed to his room to give Emery and her mum some space to talk things through and try to come up with a plan. They hadn't gotten very far, but at least now she'd told her mum the truth, and she had reassurance that it was okay for her to move back home if she needed. Most of her stuff was already back anyway; she'd been bringing a little bit more with her each time she'd come to visit over the last few months. At some point, she would need to look for work, but for now, they'd agreed the best thing for her was to take a break.

It was a quiet Sunday, with a slightly overcast sky and the smell of incoming rain drifting through the air. Danny was meeting up with a friend, and their mum was in the lounge room catching up on an old crime show that hadn't aired since she'd been their age.

Emery picked up her favourite brush. She chose a canvas from the pile, dragged out the tub that held most of her paint, set a cup of water down on the desk beside her and...

nothing.

Instead of her mind giving to the blank canvas, the canvas reached out and contaminated her mind, spreading the blankness through like mould creeping over old fruit.

She stayed like this for a while; chest growing heavier, tears threatening to spill, encumbered by feelings of doubt. Maybe she was never supposed to do this. Maybe art, as much as she loved it, just wasn't for her. She'd spent her whole life kidding herself, believing this was something she'd be able to do, something she could possibly even make a career from, but right now she couldn't even finish one stupid painting.

She was a joke.

An imposter.

Pathetic.

She was anything *but* an artist.

But it was all she'd ever wanted.

She wandered back to her bed, crawled under the covers, and curled up as tight as she could manage. The warmth and darkness muffled the world around her, protecting her from all the uncertainty of everything outside. Lights, noises, sudden movements outside the window… none of them could touch her here.

But she could still think.

A couple of hours passed before the buzzing of a phone ripped Emery from her spiralling mind. She slipped an arm out of the covers and reached over to grab it, bringing it close and opening the text as soon as she saw the name.

Laura: Hey I know this is super short notice but I heard you were in town so… I'm doing a market stall tomorrow if you wanna drop by. If you're free, of course. You could bring a few paintings down if you want, add them to the table.

Emery: Oh, of course! I think I've got a few somewhere, I'll see what I can find. Send me the info!!

It had been a while since she'd seen Laura, so Emery was excited to join her at the market. Maybe it would even do her some good to get out and see her old friends for a few hours. She clambered out her bed and began dashing around the room in search of her old paintings. Anything she found that was complete and ready was placed into an old milk crate beside the wardrobe, ready to grab and walk out without stopping to sift through them a second (or fifth) time. No opportunities to change her mind or talk herself out of it. Of course, she didn't expect the paintings to sell, but there was no harm in taking them along just in case.

***

Emery's mum dropped her off at the market early, loaded up with her crate of old paintings and a container of mixed lollies to snack on in the dull moments. The market was organised by a community centre and was set up across the empty lot beside it. Food stall operators were dashing in and out of the building in search of various necessities, a couple of community centre volunteers were plodding about with checklists and maps to give directions, and there was a musician set up in the back corner with a guitar and stool.

Admiration flowed through Emery as she glanced around. Whatever you were into, there was a stall for it. She'd strolled past a jewellery stand, a sketch artist, a couple of painters, three different crochet stalls, and so many more she hadn't gotten a proper glance at. There was even someone selling plants! Desperate as she was to stop, she continued to walk up and down the rows of stalls until she heard a scream, quickly followed by someone crashing into her from behind.

'I'm set up over here,' Laura said cheerfully. Her hair had grown out since they'd last seen each other, and it settled gently over the shoulders of her custom-made pink, white, and blue dress. 'I'm so glad you made it! Nick got a job a few weeks ago so he's always either there or trying to catch up on school work. Anyway, I've left half a table free for your paintings but if you need more than that I can bunch some stuff up a bit more.'

'Oh, I only brought a few small ones so half a table should be fine. Even if it's not, that's okay. I don't wanna mess up your display.' Emery said softly, already feeling a need to catch her breath.

'No no, it's fine. I spread everything out more than I needed to just so it didn't look empty. There's *heaps* of space.' She grabbed the crate from Emery's hands and took off towards her site, motioning for Emery to follow. Laura had two tables set up in an L shape at a corner stall. One was covered with handmade greeting cards, woven keychains, and an assortment of sticker bundles. The other table had a few miscellaneous trinkets taking up a small portion, but was otherwise vacant and waiting to be filled.

Emery started setting up her paintings while Laura ran off to track down something to drink. The smaller paintings fit perfectly on the table, and she was able to prop the larger ones up along the front. She settled down in the spare chair she'd found stashed under the table and checked the time as Laura returned and handed her a large cup of hot chocolate.

'Seems to be the right kind of weather for it,' Laura said with a smile.

'And the right kind of mood. Thank you,' Emery responded before taking a sip and letting the warmth run through every part of her. 'Your hair's getting long. They finally stop harassing you about it at school or something?'

Laura laughed. 'Actually, no. I'm finishing my final year at TAFE while I build up my business. My parents are pissed, of course, but it's not like they were ever proud to begin with. They haven't kicked me out yet, so that's something, but I'm trying to save up enough to safely move out.'

'Oh, shit yeah. TAFE would be great for you. I'm moving back home, actually, so sing out if I can help with anything.'

Laura's smile flicked slightly as she nodded in response. She didn't push for an explanation; Emery would talk about it when she was ready. Instead, they chatted for a while, catching up on everything Emery had missed while she'd been away, pausing their conversations when the occasional passerby got too close and picking up perfectly when they were free again. The market wasn't big, and it was a little out of the way, so there weren't a lot of people around. Laura spent the free time making more keychains. One of Emery's sketchbooks was in her bag, but even thinking about picking it up brought on enough anxiety to wipe out a goat.

About an hour into the market, a lady approached their stall, heading straight to Emery's side. Her hands were full with stacks of flyers, and she wore a lanyard with the local council logo printed along it.

She pointed at the paintings. 'Are these all you have?'

'Uh, they're all I have with me today. I do make other paintings though,' Emery responded quickly, taking extra care not to trip over her words.

'There's this café opening in town next weekend. They need some art for the walls, and I think something like this would be just perfect. Would you be able to do that?'

'Oh. Yeah, absolutely. That would be amazing.'

The lady fumbled her pile of flyers, pulling one out of the stack. 'This has my number on it, if I give you that, you could give me a call on Monday and we can sort out the details.'

Emery looked over the flyer for an opening event, trying to spot the phone number. She was about to point it out when the lady handed over her phone.

'Put your number in, and I'll give you a call.' She placed a copy of the other flyer, one for a sporting event, on the table with the first flyer. 'That one has my number on it. My name's Maria, by the way. Yours?'

'I'm Emery.'

'Well, thanks Emery,' Maria said as she took the phone back. 'We'll talk on Monday.'

Emery stood frozen in shock and watched as the strange lady disappeared as quickly as she'd arrived. After a moment, she slowly backed into her seat next to Laura, who was wide-eyed and grinning at the interaction she'd just witnessed.

'Well,' Emery said with an excited sigh. 'I guess I'm gonna have a painting on display.'

***

By Wednesday morning, Emery still hadn't started the painting. She needed to get it done soon. It was due at the opening event on Saturday morning and needed a protective coat before that, and she wanted the protective coat to have a day to air out, which meant she needed to do that on Thursday but the painting needed to not just be done but *dry* by Thursday, but it was already Wednesday and she *still hadn't started*.

She slumped to the floor in hopes of finding a way to soothe her spiralling brain. It was a brilliant opportunity, too good to pass up, but it was a lot. She knew she needed to start, she *wanted* to start, but the force of the demand made it feel like an impossible task. The longer she left it, the worse it got, and the more urgent it all became.

It had been like this since the market. Her mind had been in two halves, both screaming at each other. One said she needed to just start and get it over with, that she knew she needed to start, that she couldn't let this go and it would be fine if she just started. The other kept reminding her how urgent it was, and questioning if she would even be able to meet their standards. What if she did the painting and took it in and they hated it?

Emery took a deep breath and looked around the room, at all of her supplies, overflowing folders, at the unfinished work. The sketchbook she'd used a few days before still sitting on the floor. Something inside her fluttered as she stared at it, the beginnings of an idea she hadn't quite managed to uncover. She picked it up, cautious though she wasn't sure why, and turned to the page from the previous week, slightly crumpled from where she'd fallen asleep.

The piece was a mess, but it wouldn't be too hard as a starting point. *And it would be nice to see it in colour*, she thought.

Colours piled up on the desk as she dashed around the room, searching for the ones that spoke to her the most, comparing them as she went to check they were compatible. Once she'd found everything she wanted, she picked up her brush again, loaded it up with just the right amount of the perfect shade, and delicately dragged it across the empty space.

If someone had seen her in that moment, they would assume things were fine. Good. *Normal.* But Emery's insides were a fierce storm. Her stomach swirled, her thoughts spiralled, the air in her lungs was restricted.

If someone had looked at Emery as they entered the room, they would see a girl doing the thing she loved the most. They would see brush strokes and colour and creations coming to life.

But if they could see her face, they would see her tear-stained, straining, and weighed down by a thousand feelings. They would see her fighting a demon stronger than they could ever imagine. They might finally see *her*. Just like her brother, but without the words.

But slowly, she let go, allowing her movements to loosen up just a little. Her left hand served as a palette while her right held the brush as an extension of itself, sweeping strokes, tapping splotches, and carefully pricking finer details as she brought her creation to life. Over time, what had felt like a disaster waiting to reveal itself, Emery had not only finished the painting, but felt comfortable with what she'd done. Towards the end, despite the pain, hunger, and desperate need for a trip to the toilet that she hadn't been able to recognise in the midst of fixation, she'd managed to find peace and comfort again.

She'd actually... enjoyed herself.

Satisfied with what she'd created, Emery tidied up the brushes and paints and tended to the most urgent of her body's demands before collapsing on her bed and wrapping herself up under her doona. The weight of the covers and the horizontal position were comforting and rejuvenating. Sleeping wasn't the only way to recharge. Emery had been exhausted and overwhelmed before the market, and everything since had only amplified those feelings. Her entire body ached from the stress of it, and as hard as she tried, she could no longer stop the tears from running down her face.

A little while later there was a soft knock and she sensed her door opening, but she couldn't move. She heard a few footsteps and the sound of shuffling in drawers. The room darkened as the curtains drew closed. Then, slowly and carefully, an extra weight fell down across her coiled form.

'I get it,' her brother said softly. 'This blanket is the best. It's a little heavier than the others, so it kinda pushes the pressure out. I'll be in my room and I've got my phone if you need anything.'

The door closed again behind as he left, and Emery closed her eyes, focused on nothing, and let the covers pin her down as the stress slowly escaped from her body.

***

Two weeks later, after Emery had taken a proper break to recover, she decided to stop by the café and see if her work really was on display. Due to her spurt of hibernating with snacks and a pile of old DVDs from her childhood, she'd run low on a few supplies and was forced to finally resurface. The time off had done wonders though, and she was no longer at risk of breaking down after every two-minute interaction.

She ordered a hot chocolate on her way in and headed through to the main area, seating herself at one side where the light wasn't too harsh. An older lady with short greying hair delivered her hot chocolate along with a complimentary cookie. Emery thanked her before she headed back to the kitchen. Alone again, she gazed at her surroundings.

Across from her was a small bookcase, filled with an assortment of novels and textbooks. One section of the room was corned off with a few couches and a TV hooked up to a gaming console. There were a few tables in the middle, where Emery was, some complete with students on laptops. Then, at the far end, was a pool table, and beyond that, in the middle of the wall, was her masterpiece.

Air caught in her chest as everything settled into place. They actually put it up. Her work, *hers*, was on display in a café.

She picked up her things and moved to a different table, one closer to the painting, so she could see it properly in its surroundings. Its *home*. Where everyone could see it, and *wow* someone had actually *paid her* for this. Emery smiled to herself as she sipped her drink, feeling a sense of accomplishment settling loosely around her skin. She decided to stay for a while, pulling out her sketchbook and making some rough drawings while she kept half an eye on the wall.

Time got lost between her fingertips and the page, pouring pieces of herself out in subtle grey lines, and she almost missed the young girl staring at the painting. The girl called out to her friend to come have a look, and as she turned she caught Emery's eye.

'It's magnificent, isn't it?' the girl said cheerfully. A person with short multicoloured hair crashed into her and they continued to talk between themselves. 'I just wish the artist had left a social tag so I could find them online. There's nothing here. No label or anything. I wonder if they have an online store for prints.'

The voices trailed off as Emery's insides started to rush around. People didn't just like her art, they wanted more of it. It wouldn't be that hard to set up an account. She wouldn't need to pressure herself or post on a schedule either, she could just post when she had something or when she felt inspired to. Maybe it was worth a shot, just to see what happened. The worst case was that no one would notice.

Having made a decision, she finished her drink and tidied up her things to head home. She'd been to the craft store and the supermarket before the café, so she headed straight to the bus stop, timing it perfectly for the next bus home. During the trip, she set up an Instagram account and uploaded a photo of her painting in the café, tagging them in the caption to say thanks.

By the time she got home, the café had shared her post, and she had three new followers and a comment on the painting.

"Glad you made an account. Really excited to see what you do next □"

Emery smiled, finally feeling whole for the first time in months, and picked up her brush. She knew exactly what she wanted to paint.

Acknowledgements

I'd like to start by saying a massive *thank you* to everyone who ever doubted me, and especially to those who still do. Many of these stories would not exist without you. You have gifted me with a reason to push through the sticky moments in my brain, even if that reason is only to prove you wrong. Truly. Thank you.

This collection would have been impossible without my incredible friend, Kavai Masei, who proofread most of these stories for me along the way, pulling me up on typos and embarrassing little mistakes. Thank you for listening to me ramble about ideas, for putting up with my incessant info-dumping about my plans for this project (and others), and for insisting on reading every story before I posted it, not once, but *at least* twice, and often at ridiculous hours.

Thank you to both friends and enemies who, simply by existing, inspired me to write, not just these characters and stories, but many others that remain hiding in my drafts. Maybe one day they'll find the strength to crawl out into the light and you'll be able to read those too.

I don't want to get too specific here, for the sake of privacy, but I want to add a special thanks to a few people. To my Art Friend, for your endless support and encouragement, and for always sending me cat photos at the exact right moments. To the one who was *almost* a Smith, thank you, also, for the many photos of cats (and the occasional quokka), and for being encouraging even when I was being weird and vague about my plans. To the group formerly known as *The Regulars*, we don't talk as much these days, but you were a big part of this too, and I hope you never stop being yourselves.

And to the friend I've known the longest, thank you for your insight and patience while I was spamming you with progress shots of the cover.

A bonus little thank you to Shane Blackheart for saving this project from an untimely death, and me from an untimely breakdown. I'm not sure either of us would have survived without your encouragement.

Finally, thank you to my Patreon supporters for your never-ending patience while I scrambled around chaotically, dropping stories without a real schedule, and falling incredibly behind towards the end. You all deserve a medal tbh.

Blurbs and Content Warnings

The Cave

On a dark and stormy night, a girl went to deliver a letter.

Reflections

A young boy always finds himself alone when he's at the playground. Until one day, when a new girl shows up, and he finds they have more in common than he ever could have guessed.

- exclusion
- body image

The First Zombie

Fred never thought working in fast food could be deadly until an infected cut turns him into a zombie and starts the apocalypse.

- aversion to food
- blood
- death
- violence

Flicker

Late one night, she heard knocking at the door, but when she opened it, there was no one in sight. And when the knocking continued... she knew she wasn't alone.

- blood
- death

A Body of Water, Organs of Fish

While trying to get approval to start T, Nick explains the aquatic ecosystem analogy and the ways he realised he was trans while struggling to understand his feelings as an autistic person.

- body image
- transphobia
- mention of periods

A Banquet for the Outcasts

When Ash is excluded from his family Christmas get-together, he teams up with his friend to do something special for others like them. A Christmas dinner for all those who have been left out because of who they are.

- transphobia
- misgendering & deadnaming

The Pit

Someone is falling. It's getting darker. Will it ever stop?

- mental illness
- death

D(ist)ress

After a tense Christmas morning with unsupportive relatives, Nicholas finds a way to turn it around by regifting something that wasn't right for him to make Laura's day and give her the gift she deserves.

- misgendering & deadnaming

Project Milton

When Cody was seventeen, his cat died.

Ten years later, he wins an essay contest and is selected to be one of the first people to have the opportunity to bring a loved one back to life.

But a lot has changed since his cat last saw him, and Cody is afraid Milton won't recognise him anymore.

- mentions of death

Bad Parenting

Jonah hasn't heard from his mother in months. But one day she calls, asking him to meet her for dinner with her new boyfriend. It's only dinner. What could possibly go wrong?

- minor alcohol mention
- stalking
- violence
- gore
- distortion of reality
- blood

Good Friends

Aiden doesn't really get crushes, but when Imogen says she wants to date him. He doesn't think he likes her, he feels sick. Broken, perhaps. But his best friend insists he likes her back.

Not only does it lead to a date, but it might just help him find the answers he needed all along.

- misinterpretation
- kissing

To the Ground

Today I went down to the river and realised all my dreams were dead.

- disconnection to reality
- death

Consequences

Sometimes a man might believe he can do no wrong, and never facing repercussions might reinforce those ideas. But when a man's grandson dies as a result of his actions, he finds himself being haunted by the things he did, showing what can happen when your past actions get brought back and the roles are reversed.

- blood
- mentions of alcohol & alcoholism
- brief mention of suicide
- brief mention of rotting food
- vulgar language
- transphobia
- mentions of abuse

Breathe

In primary school, everyone dressed the same, but now Nicholas is starting high school, and the rules have all changed.

After how far he's come, he's suddenly forced into a dress again, and Laura is being told to cut her hair.

But then they meet Emery, who shows them there are other ways to survive (and maybe make a few friends along the way).

- misgendering

Pirates

Two brothers decide to run away and become pirates. Escaping to the water for a life of adventure sounds perfect... if only they were more organised.

From Pianos to Petals

Brendon is young, handsome, and successful. He is content with life, and doesn't feel as though he's missing anything.

But his mother disagrees. She's set out to find the perfect partner for her son, and despite his attempts to sabotage the plan, she may actually succeed, even if the outcome isn't quite what she'd expected.

This one is a gay retelling of The Princess and the Pea.

- parental meddling

Lights

Now that he's living on his own, Ash is finally able to put up lights at Christmas. He's excited to start spreading a little joy for the locals, but when he makes the decision for this to be the final year he participates in the holiday, he wonders what it might mean for the future. Is his time bringing smiles through decorations set to end as soon as it's begun?

- discussion of religion
- seasonal hypocrisy

Santa's Beard

Santa and Mrs Claus were childhood best friends, born into their roles as the bringers of Christmas joy.
Now there's a secret eating away at them. How is Santa supposed to bring joy to the world when he can't find his own?
But Mrs Claus has a plan. She's set out on a mission to go find him a boyfriend, meeting a few interesting characters along the way.

- mention of depression
- drag performers

Finding Colours

After dropping out of TAFE to recover from burnout, Emery struggles to find the motivation to do what she loves most. Even existing takes an exorbitant amount of energy in this state. But with the support of her family, friends, and a well-timed stranger, she might be able to find exactly what she needed all along.

- autistic burnout

About the author

Jake is a little cloud of chaos disguised as a human, often still trying to understand how anything works. At some point during his childhood, he figured out what words were and made an unconscious decision to obsess over them in every way possible. As a result of this, he is a songwriter, a poet, an aspiring author, keeps a spreadsheet of some of his favourite words, and has a small room filled with enough books to build a small house.

After growing up in a space that fought to hide his differences, he has opted to use his love of words for good and create worlds filled with characters who are loudly and openly themselves.